D0045897

ALSO BY ELISE ALLEN & DARYLE CONNERS

Gabby Duran and the Unsittables

First Hardcover Edition, May 2016
1 3 5 7 9 10 8 6 4 2
G475-5664-5-15319

Printed in the United States of America

This book is set in Adobe Caslon Pro
Designed by Marci Senders
Reinforced binding

Library of Congress Cataloging-in-Publication Data
Names: Allen, Elise, author. | Conners, Daryle, author.
Title: Troll Control / Elise Allen & Daryle [illegible]
Description: First hardcover edition. | Los Angeles ; New York : Disney-Hyperion, 2016. | Series: Gabby Duran and the Unsittables ; second dossier | Summary: Twelve-year-old Gabby, recruited by a secret agency to take care of extraterrestrial children, is assigned to babysit a troll.
Identifiers: LCCN 2015023591| ISBN 9781484709368 (hardback) | ISBN 1484709365
Subjects: | CYAC: Extraterrestrial beings—Fiction. | Babysitters—Fiction. | Trolls—Fiction. | BISAC: JUVENILE FICTION / Fantasy & Magic. | JUVENILE FICTION / Humorous Stories. | JUVENILE FICTION / Business, Careers, Occupations.
Classification: LCC PZ7.A42558 Tr 2016 | DDC [Fic]—dc23
LC record available at http://lccn.loc.gov/2015023591
ISBN 978-1-4847-0936-8

Visit www.DisneyBooks.com

THIS LABEL APPLIES TO TEXT STOCK

Gabby Duran

Troll Contro

ELISE ALLEN & DARYLE CONNE

Disney • HYPERION
LOS ANGELES NEW YORK

FROM ELISE TO MADDIE, ALWAYS—AND TO RAHM AND EVERETT FOR LOVING GABBY RIGHT AWAY

FROM DARYLE TO LIZ LEHMANS, WHO IS OFTEN THE ONLY GROWN-UP IN THE ROOM.

SECOND DOSSIER
Troll Control

WARNING

This book contains revelations so classified that only the most covert layers of the most secretive sects of the Worldwide International Government even know they exist. A single leak could send devastating ripple effects throughout space-time and obliterate the world as we know it.

EVEN IF YOU READ THE FIRST DOSSIER, YOU MIGHT NOT BE PREPARED FOR THE DISCLOSURES IN THIS SECOND DOSSIER. IF YOU HAVE ANY UNCERTAINTY AS TO WHETHER OR NOT YOU'RE PREPARED TO DELVE DEEPER INTO THE ONGOING FILE OF GABBY DURAN, WE MUST BEG YOU IN THE NAME OF ALL YOU HOLD DEAR...

UNDER NO CIRCUMSTANCES SHOULD YOU TURN THE PAGE

THANK YOU FOR YOUR LOYALTY.
THE ASSOCIATION LINKING INTERGALACTICS AND EARTHLINGS AS NEIGHBORS WELCOMES YOU TO PERUSE THE SECOND DOSSIER OF ASSOCIATE 4118-25125A, A.K.A. GABBY DURAN, SITTER TO THE UNSITTABLES.

chapter ONE

"Alien . . . Alien! . . . ALIEN!!!!"

Satchel Rigoletti's eyes bugged out and his long body curled into itself as his voice rose to a high crescendo of terror.

Next to him, Gabby Duran bobbed her brown curls in a nod.

"It's an alien," she agreed.

Satchel turned to her. His face was pale and his normally floppy hair stood out in all directions. "How are you not freaking out about this?" he demanded. "That guinea pig just turned into a giant, slavering, razor-toothed alien!"

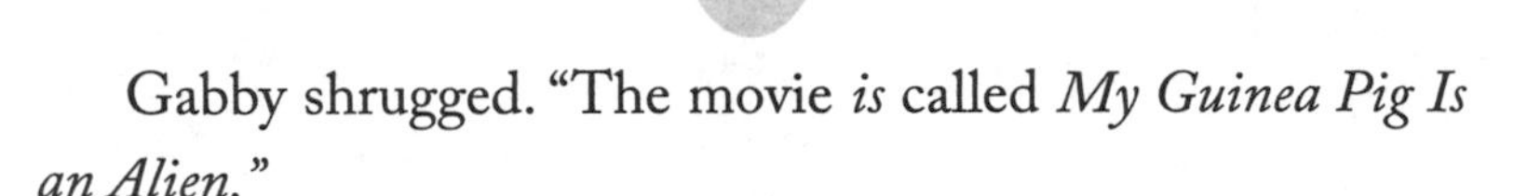

Gabby shrugged. "The movie *is* called *My Guinea Pig Is an Alien.*"

Satchel relaxed back into Gabby's overstuffed couch, and his ill-fitting 3-D glasses bounced on his face. "Yeah, but you're supposed to freak out like you don't expect it. That's what we always do."

"I know," Gabby said, adjusting her own 3-D glasses a bit. "But I'm just not buying that guinea pig as an alien."

"Interesting," said Gabby's other best friend, Stephanie Ziebeck, a.k.a. Zee. She was sitting cross-legged in front of Gabby and Satchel, but unlike them, she wasn't wearing 3-D glasses. Zee wasn't interested in cheesy action-horror flicks the way her friends were. Instead, she bent over a wild hodgepodge of metal chunks and tangled wires that she had named Wilbur. Now that Zee was on the Brensville Middle School robotics team, Wilbur came with her everywhere, and she was all about turning him into a champion.

"So what *would* you buy as an alien, Gabby?" Zee asked in an affectedly casual voice as she screwed one twisted hunk of metal into another. "Maybe . . . a *math book*?"

Satchel snorted out loud. "A math book? That is the lamest alien idea ever."

"It's not so awful," Gabby said with a smile.

Just then, the alien guinea pig on the screen shot its blaster at a giant evil rat. The rat exploded in three dimensions,

splattering virtual furry guts all over Gabby and Satchel. They screamed.

"I take everything back," Gabby gasped. "This movie is awesome!"

"Kind of weird, though, that you picked only alien movies to watch today," Zee said, still bent over her robot bits and clearly unmoved by the giant rat-splosion. "*Outer Space Outrage*, *Intergalactic Armageddon* . . . It's like you've got aliens on the brain."

"*In* the brain," Satchel clarified. "That's the plot of *Intergalactic Armageddon*. These tiny alien parasites crawl into an astronaut's ear and burrow into his head. Then, when he unwittingly brings them back to Earth—"

Zee wheeled around, her zillion blond braids snapping along with her. "Satch, aren't you the least bit curious about *why* Gabby's so interested in aliens?"

"I *know* why she's so interested in aliens," Satchel scoffed. "It's because alien movies are—" He narrowed his eyes suspiciously as he noticed the knowing smile on Zee's face. "Wait—why are you giving me that look?"

"What look?" Zee asked.

"That you-want-to-tell-me-something-I-don't-want-to-hear look."

"I don't know what you're talking about," Zee said. "I was just going to explain to you that our friend Gabby—"

Satchel clapped his hands over his ears and started singing, loudly and off-key.

"Go easy on him," Gabby said to Zee. "He doesn't want to know."

"Which makes no sense!" Zee blurted. "It's the most incredible news in the universe—literally!"

Zee was right. There was a very good reason Gabby had aliens on the brain, and it had little to do with the truly spectacular splatter-quotient they brought to their movies. Just one week ago, Gabby had learned possibly the world's most enormous secret: aliens were living on Earth, blending in, both unseen and unknown by humanity. The Association Linking Intergalactics and Earthlings as Neighbors, a.k.a. A.L.I.E.N., had shared this secret with Gabby because apparently, if there was one thing aliens on Earth desperately needed, it was great babysitting. And if there was one thing at which Gabby Duran excelled, it was being a great babysitter. Even though she was only twelve, her sitter skills were so spectacular that in addition to sitting locally, she was regularly whisked all over the globe to watch the kids of some of the world's most famous and powerful people.

Gabby's first assignment with A.L.I.E.N. had been only two days ago, and it had gotten so complicated that she'd told her friends the truth so they could help. At least, she'd told *Zee* the truth. Satchel refused to listen. He didn't do secrets

because he couldn't trust himself not to let them slip out by accident. He'd still helped, but under the express orders that Gabby and Zee keep him completely in the dark.

This made Zee crazy. It killed her scientifically curious mind that someone could have the chance for mind-blowing information and choose to ignore it, so she kept trying to goad him into asking for more than he really wanted to know.

While Satchel held his ears and sang, Zee turned to face Gabby. "So tell me this," she said, "have you heard anything from Edwina?"

Gabby quickly scanned the room. Edwina was her A.L.I.E.N. connection, and she would *not* be happy if she knew Gabby had let their secret slip. Since Edwina had proven she could pop up almost anywhere, Gabby knew it was best to look before she spoke. When she saw no sign of the older woman, she moved to the floor, crouched down by Zee's side, pushed her 3-D glasses on top of her head, and leaned so close that her dark curls brushed against Zee's blonde braids.

"I've heard nothing," Gabby said. "I thought when the Fremonts canceled for today it meant maybe I'd get an assignment from . . . you know . . . but it's already three o'clock and I haven't heard anything. I don't even know *how* I'd hear anything. Carmen always schedules my jobs, but I don't think Edwina would go through her."

"Um . . . Gabby?"

It was Satchel. He sat oddly upright on the couch, the large 3-D glasses bulging off either side of his face. His mouth hung open, and his lips trembled as he tried to form his next words.

"Is there a reason Colonel Jangschmitz is tapping the screen and calling your name?"

Gabby and Zee both spun toward the TV, whipping around so quickly that Gabby's 3-D glasses plunked back down onto her nose.

She wished they hadn't.

What she saw on the screen was *Edwina*. The woman was dressed all in black, but not in her typical suit. Instead she wore the close-fitting uniform of the movie's secret alien task force, her white hair tucked under their signature cap. It was the same uniform worn by the corporal standing just behind her in the shot. He watched Edwina patiently, as if it were perfectly normal for his fellow character to stop the scene and start speaking to a single audience member.

Tap-tap-tap!

Edwina's age-lined finger pounded on the screen again, though in 3-D it felt like she was pounding on Gabby's head.

"Gabby. *Gabby!*"

Gabby broke out of her stunned stupor to blurt, "Yes! Um . . . I'm . . . um . . . how . . . ?"

“Eloquent as usual, I see,” Edwina said, leaning over Gabby and raising an eyebrow. Edwina always stood tall, but looming out of the Durans’ wall-mounted fifty-two-inch high-definition television, the woman was a giant, no-nonsense beast.

“What is happening?” Satchel’s voice warbled nervously from the couch.

“The coolest thing ever,” Zee marveled.

Gabby scrambled for an excuse. She couldn’t let Edwina know her friends had any idea about their secret. “It’s a . . . a glitch,” she finally said, “in the streaming . . . thing.”

“The ‘streaming thing’?” Edwina glanced back toward the corporal, who snorted as if he, too, thought this was the most ridiculous explanation attempt in the world. “Honestly, Gabby, you insult me. I’m well aware of what you told Ms. Ziebeck and attempted to tell Mr. Rigoletti, and while I’m not pleased, I recognize the inherent foibles of the prepubescent mind. I also trust you will share our secret with no others, and that Ms. Ziebeck has the sagacity to keep what she knows to herself. As for you, Mr. Rigoletti, should you wish to hold on to your ignorance with impunity, I highly recommend you close your eyes, clap your hands over your ears, and recommence singing.”

Gabby didn’t turn around, but the off-key warbling behind her meant Satchel had clearly taken Edwina’s advice.

"So what's up?" Zee asked.

Edwina's ice-blue eyes bored into Zee's. The woman was old, and the high-definition screen brought out every deep crease in her skin, but the glare held such power that Zee shrank into her overalls. The message was clear: Zee was *not* part of this conversation.

"I'll make this brief," Edwina said, focusing back on Gabby, "as this is a terrible movie and I have no desire to spend any more time in it than necessary. I need you to meet me as soon as possible at 3242 Robinson Street. You'll get further instructions there."

"Okay," Gabby said. "Is there anything else I need to know? How long will I be gone? Is there anything I should bring?"

"Colonel?" The corporal behind Edwina looked terribly apologetic for bothering her, but it seemed he had no choice. "Colonel, I'm afraid I need you."

Edwina rolled her eyes and sighed heavily. "One moment," Edwina told Gabby. "I have a line."

She walked several steps back toward the corporal, then spoke in an imperious voice. "I've come to a decision. There's only one way to combat an army of alien guinea pigs: with the world's largest alien hamster ball."

Edwina shook her head, disgusted. "A hamster ball?" she asked the corporal in her regular voice. "That doesn't even

make any sense. We were talking about guinea pigs, not hamsters. How does anyone watch this garbage?"

"Beats me," replied the corporal. "Broadway's more my thing. I just do this to pay the rent." Then he straightened and saluted, going back to the script. "Aye, aye, Captain!"

The two grew smaller and smaller as they walked toward the back of their ship. Was Edwina actually leaving?

"Wait, talk to me!" Gabby pleaded, running up to the TV. "I want to know more! I have questions!" She stood on her tiptoes and put both hands on the screen. "Please!"

"Why are you hugging the television?"

The deadpan question came from Carmen, Gabby's sister. She stood at the bottom of the stairs and stared at Gabby. Carmen's alarmingly short, ruler-straight bangs did nothing to temper her look of impassive distaste.

Gabby let out a ridiculously fake laugh. "I know, right? Hugging the television—crazy! Magic of 3-D. I felt like I could touch the uniform."

"You can't," Carmen noted. "It's not real."

Gabby felt her IQ drop several points. This happened a lot around her sister. Carmen was only ten years old, but she was very literal and had little patience for things that made no rational sense. The good thing about Carmen's infallible logic was that she was far more detail-oriented than either Gabby or Alice, their mom, so she excelled at managing the

schedules for both Gabby's babysitting and Alice's catering business, plus all their financial records. According to Alice, the girls' dad had been good at those kinds of things, too, and would have been very happy to know Carmen had inherited those skills.

"Why is Satchel holding his ears and singing?" Carmen asked.

"He won't be in a sec," Zee said. She pulled a rag from one of the many pockets of her overalls and hurled it at him. He jumped and his eyes popped open.

"It's over," Zee told him loudly. "You can stop now."

"It's *not* over," Carmen said to Zee. "The movie's still on. You lied to him."

At the sound of Carmen's voice, Satchel broke out in a nervous sweat. He jumped to his feet and wiped his hands on the sides of his jeans. "Oh, hey, Carmen!" he said brightly. "You're here! That's great! Really . . . really great!"

It wasn't unusual for people to get weird around Carmen. She kind of had that effect. She wasn't big on social cues, so she didn't smile or laugh much in conversation, and her natural expression was more of a glare made to shut people down. Satchel, however, had known Carmen her whole life. Gabby knew he wasn't acting weird because of *her*, he was acting weird because he knew he shouldn't talk about what

had just happened in the movie, but he also wasn't sure he could keep it in.

"What's up, Car?" Gabby asked.

"Mom wants to know if you need snacks," Carmen answered, but her eyes had locked on to Zee's robot parts, which were still splayed out all over the floor. She raised her gaze to fix on Zee. "Your stuff is touching the Puzzle Place," she said accusingly.

The Puzzle Place was a giant refurbished dining room table. It had a permanent home at the far side of the room, and it was Carmen's official spot for her favorite activity: cobbling together one of her gazillion-piece jigsaw puzzles. To Carmen, the Puzzle Place was sacred. Nothing was allowed to touch it.

"Sorry, Car," Zee said. She stretched out to move the offending bits and pieces from anywhere near the table legs and pack them back into the camouflage duffel bag she reserved for all things Wilbur. As she did, she glanced meaningfully at Gabby. "Actually, I think we're all going to go."

Gabby's skin prickled. She'd gotten so thrown by Edwina's bizarre appearance, she'd almost forgotten the woman's order. Gabby had to go to 3242 Robinson Street. *Immediately*.

"Zee's right," Gabby told Carmen. "Puzzle Place is all yours. We've got to run."

"We do?" Satchel whined. "But what about the movie? They still have to make the giant hamster ball and . . ." He stopped himself as he noticed Zee's meaningful glare. "Oh right. Yeah. We have to go."

"I'm going to grab my stuff," Gabby told Satchel and Zee. "Meet me upstairs, okay?"

Gabby ran up the two flights to her bedroom, leaping the steps in pairs. With every bound, her body tingled with more and more excitement as the new reality of her day sunk in. By the time she got to her room, her heart was thumping, and she was grinning so wide she thought her freckles might pop off.

For the second time ever, she was getting an assignment as A.L.I.E.N. Associate Gabby Duran, official Sitter to the Unsittables.

chapter TWO

"You gotta let me come along," Zee begged.

Satchel had been so flustered from his encounter with on-screen Edwina that he'd left for home, but Zee and her giant duffel bag were sprawled on Gabby's bed as Gabby scrambled to get her things together. Gabby had already changed out of her movie-day-in-the-house sweats and was now picking through the piles of clean and dirty clothes on the floor to find her babysitting uniform: slightly baggy jeans and a long-sleeved plain-colored T-shirt. It was the perfect outfit—comfortable for running around with kids, but presentable enough for parents.

"I can't let you come!" Gabby insisted. "It's against the rules."

"So was telling me in the first place, but Edwina was cool with that!" Zee countered.

"Did you see the look on her face?" Gabby retorted. "She's not 'cool' with it, she's just not killing me for it. Or firing me. *Yet*. But she could, and then—"

"Then I'd have even less access to the aliens," Zee mused softly, sucking the end of a braid. "I see what you're saying."

Actually, Gabby wasn't saying that at all. She was going to say that without her, alien children would go back to being "Unsittable," a label given to them because alien kids were about as good with secrets as Satchel. Edwina had shown Gabby that if you looked closely enough at the news over the years, it was easy to find bizarre stories that were actually incidents of supposedly human children revealing their true alien identities to wildly freaked-out babysitters. Luckily, the sitters were rarely taken seriously, but A.L.I.E.N. couldn't count on that lasting forever. Sooner or later, the truth would get out, and Gabby had seen enough movies to know what would happen then. Dissection, warfare, world annihilation . . . Nothing good came of humans finding aliens in their midst. That was why alien kids had been declared Unsittable. If they weren't around human sitters, they couldn't blab to human sitters.

Gabby was different. She already knew their secret and had sworn to protect it. Alien parents could count on her to take care of their kids, and the kids left with her could be themselves. Gabby had meant to explain to Zee how wonderful it felt to help these aliens who needed her, but Zee's mind was already whirring down its own path.

"Fine," she conceded, "I won't go with you. Just, like, take pictures of whoever it is. Or better yet, get a blood sample. I have a microscope at home and—"

"No!" Gabby objected.

"I don't mean like at a doctor's office," Zee clarified. "You just maybe take her to a playground or someplace she might slip and scrape her knee. You fix her up, then bring me back the Band-Aid when she's all better."

"Stop," Gabby said.

"I'm just saying, this is a major scientific opportunity!"

Gabby let it go. She had picked her way over the sea of clothing mounds to her all-important purple knapsack and was sifting through it to make sure it held everything she might need. Gabby had found the knapsack in a thrift store when she was only nine, and from that minute she'd always kept it with her. It had just the right combination of large and small outer and inner pockets to perfectly fit everything she needed. In one area she kept basics like ChapStick, snacks, her wallet with her student ID and

emergency hundred-dollar bill, and her house keys. Other areas held all her babysitting tricks—the little odds and ends she'd collected over the years to make her knapsack the ultimate playground for any kind of kid. She had the pencil-top erasers she'd decorated as pinkie-puppets, the tiny notebooks filled with codes she'd created for secret spy adventures, the squeeze packets of ketchup she'd use to turn gross vegetables into bloody zombie food kids couldn't wait to wolf down, and the easy-peel cling-on hooks she could stick on walls and ceilings to help with emergency fort building.

The knapsack also held her bag of marbles. Not just any marbles: she'd found these at an amusement park shop where they sat in a giant bin, so Gabby got to pick out each one individually. She'd spent so long marveling over her options that eventually her mom left her in the shop armed with her cell phone while she took a very impatient Carmen around to rides. They'd popped back after each ride only to find Gabby still entranced by the marbles, plucking out one for its beauty, one for its geometric swirls, one for its amazing cat's-eye that seemed to look right at you . . .

In the end, Gabby had gathered thirty completely unique marbles. Since then, whenever she needed something truly mesmerizing for a kid she was sitting, she could always pull out the soft leather pouch and count on the marbles to come through.

"And you tell me *I* carry a lot around with me," Zee remarked. She had crawled to the side of the bed and leaned over it, peering into Gabby's seemingly bottomless knapsack.

"Not done yet," Gabby said. She grabbed the book she was reading for history class and added it to the mix. Always good to have study material for downtime. She'd prefer to bring her French horn to practice, but that was one item that wouldn't fit inside the knapsack.

"Did you finish your report?" Zee asked.

All the sixth graders had been working on a massive history paper since the first day of school, and it was due tomorrow. Gabby pulled out her keys and held up the purple thumb drive she always kcpt on the ring.

"Completely," she said. "Printing it up tonight."

She tossed the keys back in her knapsack, zipped the bag, and slung it over her shoulder. Zee got up and did the same with her duffel, then the two girls went downstairs.

"Hey, baby!" Gabby's mom, Alice Duran, called when they neared the kitchen. Alice's Einstein-wild hair bounced as she folded the reddish-brown, gooey contents of a giant bowl with a rubber scraper.

"Hi, Mom."

Alice stopped stirring so she could give Gabby a big one-armed hug. The hug pushed Gabby's face into Alice's stain-splotched It's All Relativity apron, but the stain

smelled amazing, so Gabby didn't mind.

"Is that graham cracker and . . . pancetta?" Gabby asked. Having a caterer for a mom had trained Gabby's nose to sniff out all sorts of bizarre flavors.

"And kumquat and cayenne," Alice added. "It'll be a cookie, eventually. I saw it on a TV show, but I want to try it out before I use it. There's a batch cooling, or you can grab one of the dark-chocolate bananas from the freezer."

"Thanks, but I actually have to go."

Gabby said it before she realized she couldn't tell Alice *why* she had to go. She couldn't say it was a babysitting job; Alice would wonder why Carmen hadn't scheduled it.

A glance at Zee's backpack inspired her. "I'm going to help Zee with her robotics stuff," she said, then immediately felt the blush crawl up her face. It was a horrible excuse. Gabby didn't know the first thing about robotics. And Zee had been working on her robot downstairs—why would they need to go someplace to do what they were already doing?

"I just need another pair of hands," Zee jumped in, reading Gabby's mind. "Basic stuff. And there's some equipment at the robotics lab that would help a lot."

"She said it might take a while," Gabby added, hoping to give herself as much time as possible for Edwina's job. "Is it okay if I have dinner with Zee?"

"It's okay with my parents," Zee said.

At least that part wasn't *entirely* a lie. Zee's parents would always say yes to Gabby eating with them. They just hadn't said yes specifically for tonight. Luckily, Zee and Gabby both knew Alice was comfortable enough with the girls house-hopping for meals that she wouldn't feel the need to call and double-check.

"Okay by me," Alice said. "Just call and let me know if you need a ride home. And no later than eight—it's a school night."

"I promise," Gabby said, already racking her brain for good excuses she could use if she had to go back on that promise. Edwina hadn't exactly given her an end time for the assignment.

Alice saw Gabby off with another hug, then Gabby and Zee bundled themselves into their jackets and ran outside. A clock ticked loudly in Gabby's head as she grabbed her bike from the garage. Edwina did *not* like to be kept waiting.

Gabby had already slung her leg over the bike and Zee was on her skateboard when the door across the street banged open to reveal the last person in the world Gabby wanted to see.

Madison Murray.

Madison had been Gabby's across-the-street neighbor forever. They were also the two brightest lights in the Brensville Middle School Orchestra. Every solo went to either Madison on flute, or Gabby on French horn. On paper

they should have been fast friends, but apparently Madison never read those papers. She had always gone out of her way to rebuff any effort Gabby made to be nice, and her main goal in life seemed to be making Gabby miserable.

"Oh, look!" Madison cried as she stalked across her yard. "It's Gabby Duran, winner of the Screech of Shame Award!"

"Screech of Shame award?" Zee asked.

"Because I missed her big H.O.O.T. decorating session yesterday," Gabby muttered. "The whole thing's owl-themed, so, you know, Screech of Shame."

"But you were working," Zee said. Then she called it out to Madison. "She was working!"

Madison flounced across the street to them, her silken shoulder-length blonde hair glistening in the afternoon sun. She wore black leggings, black boots, and a sleek sweater with a fashion scarf. Gabby couldn't imagine looking that put-together for picture day at school, never mind a Sunday afternoon at home.

"I was working, too, Stephanie Ziebeck," Madison said. She had an unpleasant habit of calling people by their first and last names. "The *entire orchestra* was working on H.O.O.T. Everyone except Gabby."

Despite Gabby's issues with Madison, and despite the fact that she really did need to come through for her babysitting clients, she still felt like Madison was right. Gabby

shouldn't have missed yesterday. H.O.O.T. was a huge deal for the Brensville Middle School Orchestra. It stood for Help Our Orchestra Travel, and it was how the group earned the ten thousand dollars they needed to go to MusicFest in Washington, D.C., each December. H.O.O.T. was different every year, with the theme chosen by the H.O.O.T. Honcho. This year the Honcho was Madison, and she'd planned a big auction that would stream live so they could get bids from everywhere.

It was a really good idea, and the list of donated auction items from everyone in town was pretty impressive. In her weekly e-mails and social media blasts, Madison even said there'd be a "Special Can't-Miss Surprise To Be Revealed Soon!" The whole orchestra had buzzed about H.O.O.T. since September, though they stopped a couple weeks ago to get ready for the Fall Concert. That concert had been held the previous Friday, and by the next morning it was again all-H.O.O.T.-all-the-time for the orchestra. The auction was Tuesday after school, and yesterday had been a full-court-press effort to decorate the gym for the big event.

"I'm sorry, Madison," Gabby said. "I really am. I feel awful about missing yesterday. If I could've possibly been there, I would've."

"Prove it," Madison sniffed. "You're not working now. I'll give you an e-mail list. You can send out reminder blasts."

The ticking clock grew louder inside Gabby's head.

"I—I can't," Gabby stammered. "I have to go."

It was as if Madison could smell Gabby's secret. Her eyes narrowed, and she leaned forward suspiciously. *"Where?"*

"Are you kidding me?" Zee exploded. "It's none of your business! Come on, Gabby. Let's go."

Zee pushed off on her skateboard, and Gabby pedaled after her, feeling jumbled inside. Madison was awful, but Gabby didn't like riding off in a huff. She always wanted to try to make things better between them. Still, Zee was right. Madison might not know about A.L.I.E.N., but she *did* know Gabby was hiding something. There was no reason to stick around and give her any clues about what that something might be.

"You know what I'd like to see Madison auction off at H.O.O.T.?" Zee asked as they rode. "Her keeping her mouth shut for an entire week. I'd pay *huge* money for that."

"I would, too," Gabby panted. "At least, as much as Carmen would let me take out of my account."

Unlike Zee, who seemed to have no problems zooming on her board with a giant duffel bag on her back, Gabby sweated and struggled as she furiously pumped her pedals.

"Thanks for riding with me," Gabby huffed, "but once we get close, I need to be by myself, you know?"

"I know," Zee said. But she didn't veer away. Then three

seconds later, she added, "*Or* I could just come with you, then casually skate around in front of the house while you go inside. That way I can get a little peek when they let you in the door."

"No peeks."

"Teeny peek."

"Zee, I can't!"

"Glimpse."

Gabby just looked at her.

"Okay, okay!" Zee relented. "I won't even get close. But call me when you're done. Or before you're done. Or if you get a selfie of you and the kid. Or if the kid licks you and you need help getting the saliva onto a slide."

"I'm hoping to avoid being licked," Gabby said, "but I promise I'll call if I need anything."

"Or come by right after. I have that forensics kit my parents got me. We can lift hair samples or fingerprints with it. Fun, right?"

Gabby rolled her eyes, then pumped her bike pedals even harder. Zee soon veered off to her own neighborhood, while Gabby continued toward her destination. She pedaled so hard her legs burned, and she inwardly hoped whatever child she was sitting didn't scare easily. Her face had to look like a tomato about to explode.

Turning onto Robinson Street, Gabby fully expected to see Edwina's long black limousine sitting in front of 3242.

It wasn't there.

What *was* there was a splintered FOR SALE sign, no cars in the garage, and an overgrown lawn. The lawn seemed to personally insult the gardener next door. Gabby noticed the way he'd pause while pruning bushes along that house's front walk to wipe his hands on his brown coveralls, run them through his salt-and-pepper hair, then send a blue-eyed glare disgustedly in 3242 Robinson's direction.

Gabby worried she'd heard Edwina wrong. Was this really where she was supposed to go?

She pulled her bike to the curb and lowered the kick-stand, then walked up the ragged rock path to the front door. The button for the bell looked rusted, and it crackled as Gabby pushed it in.

No sound.

She peered into the dusty picture windows next to the door, but they revealed only large, vacant rooms devoid of anything but cobwebs and dirt.

Gabby's phone vibrated in her back pocket. She pulled it out and saw "C. Jangschmitz" in the caller ID, which made no sense until she remembered it was Edwina's character in the alien guinea pig movie.

"Hello?"

Edwina's clipped voice chirped into Gabby's ear. "Are you going to stand there, or are you coming to work?"

“I’m here,” Gabby said. “But the house is empty.”

“Of course it is,” Edwina said briskly. “Now get into the limousine so I can give you your assignment.”

Confused, Gabby looked up and down the street again. No limousines had magically appeared along the curb or in any of the driveways. “It’s not here.”

“Not where you can see it,” Edwina sighed. “We’re a *secret* organization. Do you know how much attention a limousine would attract on a suburban street in the middle of a Sunday afternoon?”

Gabby considered mentioning that Edwina had already taken Gabby to a suburban street in the limo, and had twice pulled the giant car up to Brensville Middle School, but she thought better of it.

“Come to the backyard. Through the side gate. It’s open. Bring your bicycle.”

The phone clicked off. Gabby slipped it back in her pocket and ran to the curb. She peeked around to make sure no one else in any of the neighborhood’s cookie-cutter houses was looking her way. She didn’t want anyone to think she was breaking in. As far as she could tell, this was the perfect moment. Everyone was either inside or otherwise not around. Even the gardener next door had bent back over his work and wouldn’t notice her. She quickly grabbed her bike by the handlebars and bounced it over the weedy lawn

until she got to the side gate. The wood was warped, and a padlock sat inside the rusted metal latch that kept it shut.

An *open* padlock, Gabby realized. She slipped it out of the latch, creaked the gate wide, wheeled her bike through, then pushed the gate shut behind her.

From here she could see the side of the house and a small strip of the backyard. Certainly no limo.

"I'm here," Gabby said in case Edwina was within earshot. "Where are you?"

She rested her bike on its kickstand and walked alongside the house. When she reached its rear corner she turned to face the full expanse of backyard . . . and suddenly wondered if she'd ever have an encounter with Edwina that didn't make her feel like she was hallucinating.

The black stretch limo was sitting on the home's raised back deck, nestled comfortably between a barbecue and an outdoor dining room set.

chapter THREE

For several moments, Gabby just stared at the deck.

Nothing about it made sense. For starters, there was no reason for the deck of an otherwise abandoned and overgrown house to have a shining barbecue and a set of perfectly new-looking outdoor furniture. Given that it *did* have these things, plus a latticed wood overhang and a three-foot-high slatted railing, there was absolutely no conceivable way that Edwina's limousine could have gotten up there, let alone wedged itself snugly between the barbecue, a sofa, and several rattan chairs. But there it was.

Edwina's voice came out of Gabby's rear end. "Please

don't waste time gaping, Gabby. It's terribly poor form. Come into the car."

Gabby jumped, then yanked her phone from her back pocket. It was on speaker, even though she was positive she'd turned it off.

"On my way," she said, but the call had already ended. She returned the phone to her pocket, ran to the deck, trotted up the three stairs, then reached for the limousine's door handle . . . just as it popped open by itself.

Gabby crouched down to peer inside the car. Edwina sat in a far corner.

"Good afternoon, Gabby," she said with a slight nod.

"Good afternoon," Gabby replied. She climbed in and shut the door behind her, then sat across from Edwina, who showed no sign of having just appeared on Gabby's television screen. As usual, she wore a conservatively tailored black suit, with her hair pulled back in a severe bun. She sat stiffly upright, yet managed to look perfectly comfortable at the same time. Her wrinkles were less vivid in real life than they'd been in high-definition 3-D, but her eyes burned with just as much vigor. Looking into them made Gabby feel like Edwina held a secret joke, and somehow Gabby herself was the punch line.

"Edwina—" Gabby began.

"It is my strong feeling," Edwina said, cutting her off,

"that you're about to ask me a series of 'how' questions, including but not limited to, 'How did the limousine get here?' 'How did I get into your poor excuse for a movie?' and 'How did I know you'd be with only Mr. Rigoletti and Ms. Ziebeck when I appeared?' In the interest of time, allow me to assure you simply that the integrity of the dreck you call cinema remains unimpeachable and will be back in its original state should you do something as inexplicable as choosing to watch it again. As for the rest, and to avoid such tedious sidebars in the future, I strongly suggest you accept the following blanket statement: when you need to know something you will, and if such information is not presented in a timely and forthright manner, it's because it's unnecessary for you to have in the first place. Shall we continue?"

Gabby's mouth had stayed open for Edwina's entire speech. Now she snapped it shut.

"Very good, then," Edwina said. She reached up and pressed a button in the ceiling. "Time to go."

There was a loud *WHOOSH*, then Gabby's stomach lodged somewhere in the middle of her throat.

The limo was plummeting. Every organ and all the blood inside Gabby's body lurched upward to prove it, but somehow Gabby herself stayed seated. She shouldn't have. She wasn't wearing a seat belt. By all rights she should have been plastered to the ceiling. Yet still she didn't move. She'd have

thought more about how this could be possible, but her brain was squished to the very top of her skull. The few squashed synapses still functioning noticed that Edwina was having no issues with the drop at all. She reached into her bag, fiddled with her tablet, plucked some lint from her sleeve . . . Honestly, she looked a little bored.

Yet just when Gabby had found her larynx in her upper nasal passages and was about to use it to ask what was going on, her insides changed direction and slammed toward the back of her spine. Gabby re-navigated to find her voice.

"Did we just . . . ?" she choked.

"Drop several miles below the surface of the Earth into an underground freeway tube where we can drive at speeds that would make race car drivers' hearts explode?" Edwina asked.

"Um, that wasn't quite what I was going to ask, but . . ."

"Shame," Edwina said. "Because the answer to that would be yes."

Gabby was only mildly satisfied by this response, as it led her to even more questions. She was especially curious about the complete darkness outside the windows. Shouldn't an underground freeway tube involve safety lights of some kind? Gabby almost asked, but she imagined this would fall into the clearly quite large category of Things Gabby Doesn't Need to Know, so she didn't bother.

Suddenly, the limousine shifted direction again and rocketed straight up, hurling every cell in Gabby's body down to the soles of her feet. Her ears filled, popped, then filled and popped again until with a jolt, the car stopped. Filtered light streamed through the tinted rear windows. They were back on land.

Gabby gulped in deep breaths. She felt her heart thrum against her chest as it settled back into place. Her skin grew clammy, and she wondered if she was going into the same kind of shock she had when she met aliens for the very first time.

Across from her, Edwina laced her fingers and extended her arms long, stretching them out. "Wonderful ride, isn't it? Very bracing." She placed her palms on her black wool slacks and leaned forward toward Gabby. "Now get out."

"Okay." Gabby scooted along the leather bench seat and yanked on the door handle. It didn't budge. "It's not opening."

"That's because I don't want you to leave this limousine," Edwina said.

"But you said 'get out.'"

"Not 'get out.' *G.E.T.O.U.T.*"

"Ohhhhh."

G.E.T.O.U.T., Gabby knew, was the Group Eradicating Totally Objectionable Uninvited Trespassers. Their goal was to destroy all aliens, as well as those who helped them. The Brensville Middle School janitor, Mr. Ellerbee, had worked

for the group, and two days ago both Gabby and the little girl she was babysitting had nearly become his victims.

"Now tell me," Edwina began, straightening back to her full height, "have you noticed anyone watching you?"

Gabby reached up for one of her dark curls and ran it between her fingers as she thought. "Should I have? I mean, there's Madison Murray, for sure, but she's not . . . She couldn't be . . . *Is* she?"

Hope widened Gabby's blue eyes. It wasn't that she *wanted* A.L.I.E.N. to do something about her worst enemy in the world, but hey, if the girl was part of G.E.T.O.U.T. . . .

"No," Edwina said with a slight smirk that said she knew exactly what Gabby was thinking. "Think harder. Anyone else?"

Gabby kept working her curl as she went back through the last couple days. "I really can't think of anyone. *Is* some-one watching me? Like . . . another Ellerbee?"

Edwina snorted. "Were that the case, then Mr. Ellerbee would have been remarkably swift in using his cloning device."

"His *what*?"

"Not your concern. Suffice it to say we changed tactics with Mr. Ellerbee and met some conditions from him in exchange for his help. He will now remain affiliated with G.E.T.O.U.T., but work as a double agent. Already he has given G.E.T.O.U.T. false reports saying their suspicions

were unfounded and you've never had anything to do with A.L.I.E.N. As a result, they have officially labeled you 'Alien Unaffiliated.'"

Gabby scrunched her face. "But if I'm Alien Unaffiliated, why would anyone be watching me?"

"Because G.E.T.O.U.T. is highly unprofessional. While it uses bribery to win over helpers like your Mr. Ellerbee, it recruits its most ardent followers through the Internet and during late-night radio shows that cater to lovers of the paranormal, or K.O.O.K.S."

"K.O.O.K.S." Gabby nodded. "Got it. What does that stand for?"

"It's not an acronym," Edwina said. "I'm saying these are ridiculous people. Kooks. Crackpots. Loony birds. Those who are constantly told by society that their conspiracy theories and Armageddon scenarios are balderdash, and are therefore desperate for vindication. Despite your new classification, your name and face are still on G.E.T.O.U.T.'s encrypted Web site, where members can see it, make their own assumptions, and act accordingly."

"They have my picture on their Web site?" Gabby asked.

"Indeed."

Gabby shifted inside her puffy purple jacket. "Do you know *which* picture? Because if it's the one from fifth grade . . . I had raspberries at lunch, and one of the seeds caught in my

teeth and the guy got me just as I was scootching my tongue around to get it, so I look all mushy and weird. Like when a cow chews cud—have you ever seen that?"

Edwina raised an eyebrow. Gabby felt herself grow smaller.

"But I guess that's not the point," Gabby admitted.

"Indeed not," Edwina agreed. "The point *is*, that while you may not be in any danger, you need to remain vigilant. Should you have reason to feel you're being observed or followed by someone other than your flute-playing nemesis, subtly take their picture with your phone. We can analyze the image and decide if the person is a threat. Furthermore, as part of this added vigilance, you must never contact any of your charges outside of official babysitting duties. Is that clear?"

"Crystal," Gabby said, grabbing her phone and pulling up the Contacts screen. "So what's the best number to text you?"

"Excuse me?" Edwina asked.

"For the pictures," Gabby said. "Of any weird people I see. Shouldn't I text them to you?"

"You don't need a number," Edwina replied. "If you see anyone suspicious, just take the picture. We'll find it."

As Edwina's meaning sunk in, Gabby ran through a mental inventory of all the pictures on her phone. If A.L.I.E.N.

could check them out at will, there were a bunch she needed to delete—starting immediately with the tape-face series she and Zee took at their last sleepover.

"Are you listening, Gabby?"

Gabby shook away images of herself and Zee with tape wrapped around their heads, pulling their noses into ridiculous piggy snouts and their mouths into grotesque frowns.

"Yes!" she said.

"Good," Edwina said. "So G.E.T.O.U.T."

"Right," Gabby said, leaning forward attentively. "G.E.T.O.U.T. What about them?"

"No." Edwina rolled her eyes. "*Get out*. Of the car."

"Oh!"

Gabby blushed, then pulled her knapsack over her shoulder and pushed open the now-unlocked limousine door before climbing out into the glaring sun. After the dark tunnel and shaded car, she had to blink several times before she could focus. Once she did, she gasped with delighted awe.

"Oh, wow! It's like a fairy tale!"

"Fairies tell horrible tales," Edwina clucked as she followed Gabby out of the limousine. "They don't believe in plot on their planet. Chapters and chapters of nothing but flowery description. It's a nightmare."

Alien-fairy storytelling skills aside, the vista before Gabby's eyes was almost impossibly charming. The limo

had pulled up next to an arched stone bridge that straddled a gorgeously clear bubbling creek and formed the perfect frame for the lush green hills on either side. A long, cobbled path ran by the creek's bank, then disappeared around one of the hills, as if taunting Gabby with unimaginable delights just beyond her view.

Gabby turned to Edwina for direction. The older woman extended an arm and nodded.

"By all means."

Gabby took her time walking along the path, delighting in the crunch of her purple canvas sneakers against the grass that poked up between cobblestones.

"This is where he lives?" she asked Edwina. "Or . . . *she* lives? I mean, the . . . you know . . ."

"Child from another planet?" Edwina asked. "It's all right, you can say it out loud. It's a secluded area. The aliens are the only ones who live here."

Gabby's eyes widened, and everything around her became instantly twice as magical. She thought about her most recent A.L.I.E.N. clients, Wutt and Philip, and how amazing it would have been if she could have run around and played with them out in the open, without the fear of anyone dangerous recognizing their identity. Her heart pounded again, but this time with excitement. She smiled, seeing so clearly in her head what she'd find when she turned the

corner. A fantasy village, dotted with tiny hobbit houses with lush lawns where little aliens of all sorts would race around playing tag, rolling down hills, chasing puppies . . .

Then she made the turn.

Gabby rubbed her eyes, positive they weren't working correctly.

The vista in front of her wasn't what she'd imagined at all. The green hills, bubbling creek, and cobblestone path were all littered with enormous, iceberg-size objects that Gabby recognized, but were so out of place on this field that she felt as if she'd wandered into a postapocalyptic nightmare. She saw large airplanes stuck nose down, or tossed on their sides with their landing gear pointed fruitlessly into the air. She saw an ancient ship the size of her school half-buried in the ground, its tattered sails blowing in the breeze. She saw a bronze statue head tilted on its ear. It was so huge that even from a distance Gabby could tell its eye was larger than her entire body.

And all that was only the beginning. The area was strewn with so many strange and titanic items that Gabby couldn't begin to take them all in. It looked like a giant the size of a mountain had picked up an entire city as if it were a toy box, then turned it upside down and dumped out all the contents.

"What happened here?" Gabby gasped.

"The long answer to that would be slightly different

for each item," Edwina said. "The short version is a single word: Trolls."

"Trolls?" Gabby asked. "Like, the little dolls with the goofy hair and the naked butts?"

"Ideally no," Edwina said. "I generally try to avoid any nude posterior-sharing with those we serve. Real Trolls came here many centuries ago from their home planet. Unlike your previous charges, Trolls can pass for humans without disguise. They go to human schools, work at human jobs, and hold lofty positions in human industries. Yet, like other aliens, Troll children tend to save their most unrestrained and most clearly otherworldly behavior for babysitters. Hence the need for you."

Edwina clopped farther down the cobblestone path, but Gabby barely noticed. She'd spotted something on the closest oversize relic. It was a two-propeller plane, old and rusted, with holes in its side where chunks of metal had been ripped away. The plane lay tilted on the ground, balanced on one wing and one wheel. There was something scrawled on the hull, scratched in shaky block letters as if it were carved with a knife. Gabby moved closer until she could make the letters out.

Earhart.

Gabby's skin tingled.

"Edwina! Edwina!" She ran to catch up with her, then

grabbed her sleeve. "That plane . . ." she panted. "It says . . . It's not . . . I mean, it can't be . . ."

"The plane of aviatrix Amelia Earhart, missing since 1937? Indeed it is. Now please unhand my jacket. Your fingers are sweaty and the fabric requires dry cleaning."

Gabby let go but kept gaping at Edwina. "How is this not shocking to you? Amelia Earhart's disappearance is one of the greatest mysteries, like, ever!"

"It's not a mystery at all. The plane was stolen by a Troll. As for Amelia herself, she was so mortified that she couldn't solve the Troll's riddle, she went back to her home planet without a word to anyone. Except A.L.I.E.N., of course. We had to stamp her intergalactic passport."

"Amelia Earhart was an alien?!" Gabby gaped.

"From the planet Blargh." Edwina sighed. "Lovely place. Hideous name."

Gabby's head swirled. "I'm sorry—is any of this supposed to make sense to me? Because it really doesn't. At all."

"Then allow me to explain. Trolls, as I said, blend in reasonably well with humanity. However, they have some . . . foibles. Chief among these is that they steal."

"They steal *planes*?! And ships?! And big, giant statue heads?!?!"

Edwina looked forward in the direction where Gabby was gaping. "Ah," she said. "That would be the Colossus of

Rhodes. One of the Seven Wonders of the Ancient World. Tallest statue of its day. Toppled in an earthquake in 226 BC. The pieces were deemed 'lost' in 654 AD."

"But they weren't lost?" Gabby asked.

Edwina gestured to the Colossus's grim-set lips. "Does he look lost?"

Gabby didn't quite know how to answer that. After all, the statue was missing the rest of its body. Or maybe the pieces were just strewn elsewhere among the hills.

"Come," Edwina said. "I'll show you the highlights while we walk. We're expected. We don't want to be late."

Gabby trailed Edwina along the cobblestone path. As they passed each gargantuan, hulking item, Edwina explained its history. Gabby almost felt like she was on a school field trip, but one jumbled together with a tumble down the rabbit hole and a fever dream.

"On your left, you'll see the USS *Cyclops*," Edwina said, gesturing to an impossibly huge aircraft carrier sprawled on its side, "a five-hundred-and-twenty-two-foot carrier ship that disappeared in the Bermuda Triangle in 1918. Up here to your right—oh, these are interesting." She gestured to a group of tiny, weatherworn, log-and-shingle houses. "Homes from the Lost Colony of Roanoke, Virginia. Disappeared without a trace around 1587. Historians today expect foul play, of course, but the colonists actually became quite

friendly with the Trolls who stole their homes. With their help, the colonists traveled to a far more comfortable place than colonial America, I promise you that."

Gabby's brain was reaching maximum capacity for inconceivable.

"So wait," she blurted. "You're saying every missing thing from every time ever was stolen by Trolls and is right here?!"

"Don't be ridiculous," Edwina clucked. "Only *most* every missing thing from every time ever was stolen by Trolls. And the only ones here are the items stolen by the single family of Trolls who live in this area, and the long line of their direct ancestors. Other Trolls have their own treasure troves. And of course right now you're only seeing the larger items. They keep their smaller treasures closer at hand."

"But I don't understand," Gabby said, shaking her head. "Why is A.L.I.E.N. okay with Trolls taking things?"

"Diplomacy requires compromise, Gabby," Edwina said. "Stealing is the Trolls' greatest pleasure. Plus they always give their victims a fair shot. Trolls can only take something if they ask for it first, and the original owner always has the chance to get their item back by correctly answering a riddle the Troll must provide."

Gabby looked around at the very full field of stolen behemoths. "I'm guessing no one ever answered this family's riddles correctly."

Before Edwina could answer, Gabby realized something. "Google Earth!" she blurted.

Without slowing her gait, Edwina turned and raised an eyebrow. "Is that supposed to mean something to me, or will you be spouting non sequiturs as we walk?"

"It's not a non sequitur!" Gabby insisted. "With Google Earth you can see satellite images of everything on the planet! This is a giant field of massive, enormous things that everyone in the world wants to see. How does nobody know they're here?"

"Honestly, Ms. Duran, if after everything you've seen, you don't think A.L.I.E.N. can handle a little cloaking device, I'm highly disappointed in you." Edwina stopped in her tracks. "Ah. Here we are."

Gabby tore her eyes from the wonders all around and focused on where Edwina was looking. They had neared the end of the cobblestone path and stood in front of a large house with a rounded roof and dappled stone façade. The home seemed to sprout out of the lush, hilly green meadow around it. It was an island of adorable in the middle of a sea of bizarre.

Edwina looked sternly down at Gabby. "Remember," she said, "you now know what Trolls do. If you value your belongings, you will not let the Trolls steal from you. Should you mistakenly do so, A.L.I.E.N. cannot intervene. You'll

either have to answer the Troll's riddle, or lose your possession forever. If you don't wish to take that risk, let me know now. I'll cancel the appointment, and, for the time being, the Troll child will return to the ranks of the Unsittables."

The very word made Gabby flinch. Gabby's own sister had been considered "Unsittable," but it was only because Carmen was different. Gabby had been little then, but she still remembered how much it hurt every time another sitter railed to Alice about Carmen's "faults," and why those were the reasons she was never coming back.

Gabby stood taller and adjusted her knapsack on her back. "I'm taking the job," she said. "Let's go in."

chapter FOUR

As Edwina knocked, Gabby couldn't help but smile. Despite all the weirdness, nothing fired her up like meeting a kid for the first time. It was one of her favorite parts of being a babysitter. To Gabby, every kid was a puzzle-locked box. If you were interested in them enough to figure out the puzzle, you could open that box and completely connect with the person inside. From there, everything else was easy. Gabby couldn't wait to get started with the young Troll. Besides, the house was so cute Gabby could almost smell the gingerbread and apple cider she just knew were waiting inside. Maybe there'd be a pie in the oven, too, and

Gabby could take it out and let it cool on the windowsill when it was done.

Just as Edwina lifted her hand to knock again, the door swung open, and Gabby saw a thick, lumpy pickle of a nose. The nose was attached to a middle-aged woman—a Troll, Gabby assumed—but the appendage was so immense that Gabby couldn't yet take in anything else. Still, she smiled wide and strode to the door with her hand extended, ready to introduce herself like she would to any new client.

"Oh, it's you," the nose—that is, the woman—muttered. "I suppose you should come in."

The Troll woman turned her back, leaving Gabby's introduction to dry up in her throat. Gabby looked up questioningly at Edwina, but she was already walking in. Gabby followed.

The minute she entered, her visions of cider and gingerbread burst. Though the house was a large, charming cottage on the outside, inside it was more like a giant squirrel's den. The main room stretched up through the entire three stories of the home, bending in organic curves like a tree trunk. An *inside out* tree trunk, since the walls were thickly ridged and knotted like bark. Large outcroppings jutted here and there, many tufted in eye-popping shades of fuchsia, lime, or solar flare–orange upholstery. Gabby also saw several large holes in the walls. They looked like mine-shaft openings, and Gabby

wondered if the house was really just a main corridor that led to a network of tunnels.

In front of Gabby, the floor was littered with giant haystack-tangles of what looked like junk, but from what Gabby had learned outside, she assumed these were piles of smaller items the Troll family and their ancestors had stolen over the years. The mounds littered almost every space, leaving room only for a few wide walking paths and what had to be a mostly buried kitchen. Gabby half-wanted to sift through the piles and Google the contents against any long-missing treasures, but that wasn't why she was here. Instead she turned to the Troll woman, smiled, and again offered her hand.

"Hi, ma'am," she said. "I'm Gabby Duran. It's wonderful to meet you."

The woman wrinkled her large nose like she smelled something bad. She looked at Gabby's outstretched hand, then at Gabby's face. She leaned so close that her thick mat of frizzy hair tickled Gabby's cheeks, and Gabby could see every double- and triple-humped mole on her face. Then the Troll scrunched her single, protruding eyebrow, locked her black beady eyes on Gabby's, and snorted dismissively.

"This the best you got?" she asked Edwina.

Gabby was surprised by the question, but wouldn't let herself be thrown. She kept her hand out and continued, "I'm really happy you asked me to babysit today, ma'am. I promise

your child will be in excellent hands, and he'll have a great time while we're together."

"I didn't *ask* you to babysit," the woman said. "I was forced."

She turned her back on Gabby and shuffled to the wall. Then, to Gabby's amazement, long, thick claws burst out of her fingertips and bare toes. Using these fierce appendages, she scaled the wall, her claws digging into tiny grips in the ridged wood. She pulled herself into one of the tunnel holes and disappeared inside, but she couldn't have gone far. Gabby could hear the woman rummaging around.

"Allynces, it was hardly a matter of force," Edwina called up to the Troll. "You needed a sitter, I have a sitter. That's it."

Items came flying out of the tunnel hole. Gabby dodged to avoid them as they rained down. She saw a rusted 1970s curling iron, an array of plastic brushes decorated with cartoon characters, and an ivory comb covered in ancient Egyptian hieroglyphics.

Allynces emerged from the tunnel holding a large mirror, which she hung on the wall, and a wide-toothed hair pick. Staring at her reflection, she proceeded to give the matted frizz on her head slightly less mat and significantly more frizz.

"We *could* just bring Trymmy with us tonight," Allynces said. "Then we'd avoid this unpleasantness."

Was Gabby "the unpleasantness"?

"You absolutely could," Edwina said.

Allynces sighed. "No. We all agreed no kids tonight." She applied a thick layer of bright purple lipstick and eye shadow as she glared down at Gabby. "I just wish you'd given me a picture first. I mean, look at her. She's not easy on the eyes."

"I'm . . . what?" Gabby stammered.

A loud beeping sound came from Edwina's black bag. "That's me," Edwina said. She unclasped the bag, pressed something inside, then snapped the bag shut again and called up to Allynces, "Have a good night!"

With that, the older woman clopped to the door. Gabby scurried after her.

"Edwina," she said in a low voice, "I know I said I'd take the job, but maybe it's not a good idea. I mean, it doesn't sound like Allynces likes me very much."

"Did I not mention that Trolls can be brusque?" Edwina asked. "That's just their way. They assume they're a million times smarter than any human, and most of the time they're right. You just do your thing, and Allynces and Feltrymm will take you home after dinner. By eight, your mother said?"

"Yes, but . . . Wait. How did you know?"

Edwina raised an eyebrow, and Gabby knew she shouldn't have asked. "Okay, forget that part," she agreed. "But did you say *they're* bringing me home?"

"Indeed," Edwina said. "Have a good night."

She walked out the door, leaving Gabby for the first time ever in a house where she didn't feel wanted. Gabby considered slipping out and running back home, but she had no idea where home was from here. Besides, things would have to be a lot worse than this before she'd run out on a job.

Clanks and jingles drew Gabby's attention back to Allynces. The Troll woman's claws were out again, and she was crawling back down the wall. She had clearly accessorized while Gabby was talking to Edwina; the clangs and clinks were a discordant array of necklaces, bracelets, and earrings. As Allynces got closer, Gabby noticed the earrings looked like ancient gold doubloons. She'd seen similar ones at the mall, but Gabby still kind of wondered if these were the real deal.

"So . . . what can you tell me about Trymmy?" she asked Allynces, trying again for polite conversation. "Does he have any favorite foods, favorite games, fav—"

"Trymmy doesn't need help from a human," the Troll snapped. "You're here only in case of emergency, in which case your sole duty is to stomp three times on that round tile hatch and get him securely into the Holobooth, while you remain here to fight off any danger on your own."

As Allynces retracted her claws and slipped into high heels she pulled from another pile, Gabby replayed her last

sentence to see if she could translate it to anything that made sense.

It didn't work.

"Did you say 'hollow booth'?" she asked.

Allynces sighed deeply, then tilted her head and yelled to the upper reaches of the house, "Feltrymm, Edwina sent us one that can't hear!" Then she turned back to Gabby.

Gabby wasn't the tallest girl in her class by any stretch. She only came up to her mom's chest, she was shorter than Satchel, and she was only an inch taller than Zee, all of which meant most adults still towered over her. Allynces, however, even in high heels, had to grab a red upholstered footstool from beneath a hodgepodge of throw pillows, then stand on it to look Gabby in the eye.

"HO-LO-BOOTH," she sounded out.

Gabby winced. She dreaded asking another question, but if this was her main duty, she wanted to be sure she had it right. "And the round tile hatch?" she squeaked.

Allynces rolled her beady eyes, snorted a blast of hot breath into Gabby's face, then strode off the footstool and across the room. She kicked aside a pile of board games, including one chess set that looked like it was carved out of jade, and another covered with figures shaped like U.S. presidents. Once they were out of the way, Allynces pointed to the hatch. It was a single circle of black, made of nothing Gabby could

imagine, because it was so incredibly dark that it seemed to suck Gabby in. She had the horrible feeling that if she ever did step on it, the thing would pull her down like a black hole, stretching her deep into an eternity of nothingness.

Gabby felt hypnotized looking at the circle, and realized she was slowly moving closer, which was the last thing she wanted to do. She shook her head to break out of the daze, then stepped away.

"Of course," Gabby told Allynces. "Sorry I missed it."

She told herself that once Allynces and Feltrymm were gone, she'd push the board games back over the hatch.

"So." Allynces crossed her arms. "Trymmy knows where everything is, including his dinner. He can watch one hour of satellite broadcast, but *only* from LR-47, nothing Earthly. If he'd prefer to stay in his room until we return, that's fine with us. We'll be home at seven thirty on the dot, so please be ready. We'll want to get you out of here as quickly as possible."

"Yes, ma'am," Gabby said.

"Here I come, Allynces!"

The deep voice boomed from above. Allynces looked up, and for the first time Gabby saw the woman smile. Gabby followed her gaze to a tall, stocky figure with extra-thick claws scurrying down the wall with acrobatic speed and grace. Ten feet above the ground he hurled himself backward, turned a

somersault, and landed directly in front of Allynces. His back was to Gabby, but she could still see the ends of the rose he held in his mouth. He retracted his claws, then with a flourish, he presented the flower to his wife. "For you."

Allynces blushed as she accepted the rose, and Gabby couldn't help but smile. Allynces might not be the nicest being Gabby had ever met, but she and Trymmy's father were clearly in love. It made Gabby feel warm inside, and also a little sad. Her mom always said she and Gabby's dad had been in love like that, but Gabby's father had gone missing in action and was presumed dead when Gabby was only two. She wished she could have seen her own parents act like Trymmy's. Except maybe without the claws.

Allynces pointed over Feltrymm's shoulder. "The sitter."

Feltrymm turned toward Gabby . . . and his wide smile curled into a disgusted sneer.

These Trolls were going to give Gabby a complex.

Like Allynces, Feltrymm had wild dark hair that stood out in every direction. His brow was thick and rippled, and an underbite jutted his bucked-out lower teeth over his fleshy lips. Yet all of that was nearly eclipsed by his thick, pockmarked tuber of a nose. For just a second Gabby imagined he and Allynces kissing, and the careful nasal choreography that would have to happen before such an event could occur.

"Gabby Duran, I believe?" Feltrymm asked. He held out

his hand, which at that moment felt to Gabby like the nicest thing anyone had ever done for her. She shook it and smiled.

"Wonderful to meet you, sir."

"Call me Feltrymm." He remained smiling as he released her hand, but Gabby noticed he held his arm away from his body, like he'd pulled the limb out of a deep vat of sludge. "I'm sorry," he said. "Do you mind if I . . ."

He let the sentence trail as if Gabby would fill in the rest. She had no idea what he was asking, but she nodded to tell him whatever it was, it was fine by her. He smiled gratefully, then rummaged through a tall pile of what looked like hotel toiletries until he pulled out a bottle of hand sanitizer. He poured it liberally over his hands and forearms, then rubbed them together so vigorously Gabby thought he might make fire.

"We should go, Allynces," Feltrymm said, gently taking her elbow. "We're running late."

"Love you, Trymmy!" Allynces called up into the house. "Your sitter's here if you need her, but I'm sure you'll do fine on your own. If you do come down, don't look directly at Gabby after dinner. I don't like when you see scary things too close to bedtime!"

"Really?" Gabby blurted.

She clapped her hands over her disobeying mouth, but Allynces hadn't heard. She and Feltrymm had already slipped down a back tunnel. Since the two were taking Gabby home

that night, Gabby sincerely hoped the tunnel led to a garage and not some alien-black-hole-molecule-mixer-upper transporter device.

With the Troll couple gone, Gabby was alone. Well, alone except for Trymmy, who'd been told he could spend the entire night in his room if he wanted. She'd much rather the two of them hang out, but she didn't want to push it in case he felt the same way about humans as his parents did. Instead she made herself comfortable. She slipped off her purple knapsack and jacket, placed them in a clear spot against the wall, then pulled her phone out of her back pocket and texted Alice to say things with Zee were going great and she planned to be home by eight.

"YAAAAAAAA!!!!!!"

The bloodcurdling scream came from high above. Gabby's skin leaped. She looked up, and froze in absolute terror.

A young boy—Trymmy, it could only be Trymmy—hurled himself headfirst out of a tunnel near the ceiling.

"NO!" Gabby screamed. She raced into the middle of the floor and held out her arms, hoping against hope that she could somehow catch him before he smashed into the floor.

Then Trymmy's scream turned to hoots of howling laughter, and Gabby immediately relaxed. She was wrong. Trymmy wasn't falling, he was *descending*. His finger and

toe claws were extended, and he hurtled down the wall like a high-speed mountain goat. His mouth spread in a grin, and he looked so happy that Gabby smiled, too. Once he got low enough, he threw himself flat against the wall and rolled down to the bottom. He kept rolling across the floor, barreling right over the strewn toiletry bottles, board games, and throw pillows, then bounced to his feet right in front of Gabby. He spread his arms and leaned his chest forward like an alpha ape.

"That was amazing!" Gabby cheered.

Trymmy scrunched his face. "You're not freaked-out?"

"Should I be?" Gabby asked.

"Most humans are."

Gabby shrugged. "Then I guess I'm not most humans."

Trymmy narrowed his eyes and studied her, which gave Gabby a chance to look at him, too. From a distance, he looked like a totally normal human kid. Gabby pegged him at about ten years old. He was maybe a head shorter than Gabby, though his high corona of curly black hair gave him another six inches. He wore dark blue jeans and a blue-and-red-striped cotton polo top with a white collar.

At closer glance, Trymmy still seemed human. Yet like his parents, he looked like a very *unique* human. His brow was slightly raised and thickened. Gabby could imagine that one day it would stick out as much as his dad's. He had a

full caterpillar unibrow, and while at first his face seemed dotted with freckles, Gabby realized it was actually covered in moles. Some of the moles lay flat against Trymmy's skin, while others bloomed out like mini pacifiers. His nose was wide, flat, and so long that the tip of it hung over his top lip. If he really tried, Gabby imagined he could reach the ends of either nostril with his tongue. He wore thick glasses that did him the favor of magnifying his eyes. Without them, his eyes would have been far too tiny for his face. His body was small and wiry, with arms and legs just enough longer than expected that Gabby had to blink hard to make sure she wasn't imagining it.

"You're *sure* you're not like most humans?" Trymmy asked.

"Pretty sure," Gabby said. "I mean, I guess I haven't met most humans. Have you?"

Trymmy didn't answer. Instead he pegged Gabby with a steady gaze as he leaned his head to the left. After a moment, gravity forced one of his larger moles to droop over his mouth. Trymmy caught it between his teeth and worked his jaw gently back and forth, wiggling the trapped mole up and down.

Gabby knew he was trying to disgust her, but it wasn't working. She kept her eyes on Trymmy's as she curled her own tongue in on itself then stuck it out still rolled, so it looked like a tongue taco.

“Ew.” Trymmy backed away. “That’s disgusting.”

“Is it?” Gabby asked. “Or is it just different?”

Trymmy raised his unibrow. “You intrigue me,” he said. He nodded to her jacket and knapsack, sitting neatly on the floor. “Can I take your things for you?”

Gabby almost said yes, but then she remembered what Edwina told her about Trolls and their stealing habit. “No thanks.”

“Did someone tell you not to let me take stuff?” Trymmy asked. “Or are you smart enough to just know it?”

“Someone told me,” Gabby admitted, “but that doesn’t mean I’m not smart.”

“You’re not as smart as a Troll,” Trymmy said. “No human is. Did you know I’m five grades ahead of everyone else in my class at math?”

“I did not know that.”

“It’s true.” Trymmy raised his chin triumphantly. “They don’t even keep me in class with them for it. I have a special tutor and everything.”

“Then maybe you could teach me,” Gabby said. “I’m horrible at math.”

“I could try, but you probably wouldn’t keep up. Truth is, humans can’t do half of what Trolls can do.”

“You think?” Gabby said. “Try me. Just not at math.”

“Okay.” Trymmy held his hands in front of his chest.

He'd retracted his claws before, but now he shot them and his toe claws back out again. He grinned. "Follow the leader?"

Trymmy scaled halfway up the wall with gecko-like ease, then circled around so that he was looking right at Gabby. "You coming?"

Gabby pursed her lips and took a deep breath. Just like Trymmy, she held her hands in front of her chest. She squeezed her eyes shut and tensed her muscles so hard she started shaking.

"What are you doing?" Trymmy asked.

With a *whoosh,* Gabby released her breath. She let her shoulders slump and shrugged up to Trymmy. "I tried," she said, "but my claws aren't coming out."

Trymmy laughed.

"I wish they would," Gabby said, "'cause climbing looks like fun. But I guess you're right. Humans can't do half of what Trolls can do."

"Told ya so," Trymmy said.

"But I have some fun stuff we both can do." She walked over to her knapsack. "Now I'm not saying you can *take* any of these things, but we can *play* with anything you want."

Gabby plopped down on the floor, crossed her legs, and started pulling items out of her knapsack and laying them out on her jacket. She did *not* want her treasures to get mixed up with the other piles of random objects in Trymmy's house.

"Let's see, there's pencil pinkie puppets . . . super-secret-code notebooks . . . glow in the dark sticker sheets . . . Oooh, the big bouncy rubber-band ball . . ."

Gabby pretended not to notice as Trymmy slowly climbed back down the wall and edged closer and closer, subtly checking out each treasure over Gabby's shoulder as she laid it out.

"What's that?" Trymmy asked. His voice came from *right* behind Gabby now. She smiled to herself but kept her voice casual. She didn't want to spook him. She wanted *him* to be the one who chose to play. She didn't even look him in the eye when she turned to see where his finger was pointing.

Gabby grinned when she realized. Of course.

"These?" she asked, picking up the very familiar soft leather pouch. "They're the coolest thing I've got."

Gabby spun around on her rear end, held the bag in cupped hands, and raised them to the level of her nose as she looked up at Trymmy. "Want to see?"

Trymmy sucked in his large lower lip, and Gabby saw his magnified eyes dance. She felt his excitement as he reached for the gathered top of the pouch and pulled it open. Gabby's knees bounced up and down with anticipation while she waited to see what he'd say. Gabby never told kids what the marbles were; everyone she showed had their own idea.

The wait was killing her. She almost squealed as he

poked through the marbles, taking some out and swirling them around in his hand.

Finally, he spoke. "These are *so cool*."

His voice was reverent, like he'd just discovered the key to life, the universe, and everything.

"What do you think they are?" Gabby asked.

"You know what they are! They're secret mega orbs! They give you superpowers so you can do battle with each other!" His eyes grew even larger and he smiled wide. "You want to play?"

Gabby was sitting on the ground, but she felt like she was floating on air.

She'd cracked Trymmy's puzzle-lock. She was in.

"I'd *love* to play."

chapter FIVE

"How does the game work?" Gabby asked, jumping to her feet.

"They're *your* secret mega orbs," Trymmy said. "You should know."

"Right," Gabby agreed, "but, you know, house rules and all, so . . . how do *you* play?"

"Okay," Trymmy began, and his whole body came alive with wild gestures as he described the rules. His larger moles bounced with all the motion. "We each pick three secret mega orbs, but we don't let the other one see. Then we each hide one in our fist and count three . . . two . . . one . . . go!

We show 'em at the same time, and we see who wins!"

"Awesome!" Gabby's curls bounced. She was picking up on Trymmy's energy and moving around as much as him. "But how do we know who wins?"

"Ga-*bby*," he groaned and rolled his eyes. "You *know* what wins. Mostly red orbs are fire, mostly blue ones are water, and the black-and-whites are wind. Water defeats fire, fire defeats wind, wind defeats water. Got it?"

"Got it."

"Okay, now pick your mega orbs."

Trymmy smacked his hands over his glasses so Gabby could choose her marbles. She plucked out three, then held the pouch out to Trymmy. "Your turn."

"Cool," Trymmy said. *"Don't look."*

Gabby tucked her head down and curled her arms over her face so Trymmy would know she wasn't looking, but she was dying to peek. She would have loved to see his focus as he pored over each marble to make sure he chose just the right ones. But that would have broken the rules, and then he wouldn't want to play with her anymore. She had to settle for her imagination.

"Ready," he said. "Let's play."

Gabby snapped open her eyes. Without even looking, she slipped a marble into her right palm, closed her fist over it,

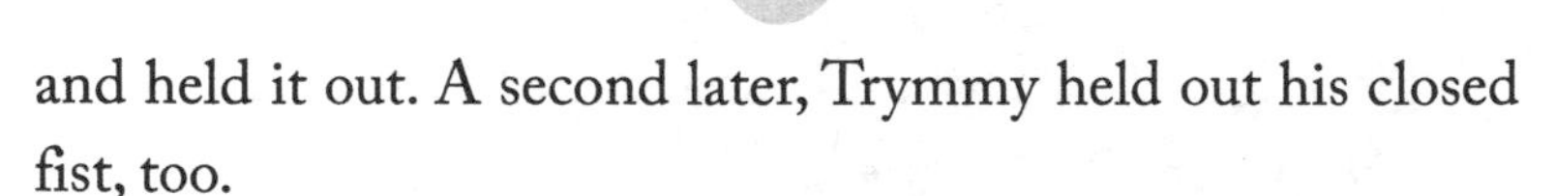

and held it out. A second later, Trymmy held out his closed fist, too.

"Three . . . two . . . one . . . go!" Trymmy cried.

They both opened their hands. Trymmy looked down at his red marble with the yellow flare in the middle and shouted, "Fireball power! Fireballs swirl in my hands and shoot across the room to you!"

Looking down at her own white marble with black specks, Gabby cried, "Wind power! I hold my arms up and spin in a circle faster and faster"—which she did—"then *zoom* it right to you!" Gabby lunged toward Trymmy, hurling the "tornado" his way.

"But my fire sucks up the oxygen in your tornado and turns into an inferno! I win!"

Gabby clutched her heart and fell dramatically to the ground. Trymmy laughed. "Okay, get up get up get up," he said. "We're going again."

They played a few rounds, and each time they acted out their power so dramatically that Gabby was out of breath and sweaty. She had just realized she should probably make him take a break for dinner, when he said, "Okay, so are you ready to play?"

"Another round?" Gabby asked. "Sure!"

"No, I mean *play*. For real. Troll-style."

He waggled his unibrow and Gabby laughed. "I thought we *were* playing Troll-style."

"Uh-uh. For that we go into the Holobooth."

He pointed across the floor at the inky circle. Even half hidden by the board games Gabby had pushed back over it, the thing's inky blackness filled her with a dread that was so elemental she couldn't even explain it.

"The . . . Holobooth?" Gabby squeaked.

She'd tried to keep the nerves out of her voice, but Trymmy obviously heard them. His nose seemed to slide even farther over his mouth, and all his moles drooped downward. "You do *want* to keep playing with me, right?"

"Yes!" She said it immediately and forced a smile back onto her face. No matter how much the Holobooth freaked her out, it couldn't really be dangerous, right? After all, it was just some unknown alien technology that made Gabby feel like her soul was being sucked away every time she looked at it.

Gulp.

The happiness on Trymmy's face helped make it better. "Cool! So to open the Holobooth—"

"Stomp on the round tile hatch three times," Gabby finished. "Your parents told me."

Trymmy nodded. Unlike Gabby's curls, his didn't bounce when he moved his head. They remained fanned straight out.

"They kind of also told me it was meant for emergencies,"

Gabby noted. "Are you really allowed to play in there?"

Trymmy rolled his eyes. "It's a safe place to *hide* in emergencies, but that's not what it's *for*. It's for games, I promise. Open it!"

With measured steps, Gabby moved to the hatch. She leaned back and kicked out a sneaker-clad foot to move the board games away from it. Once again she had the stomach-sinking feeling that the blackness was a vacuum, ready to pull her down. She didn't want to step on it. She didn't want to be anywhere near it.

She shut her eyes and stomped. Once . . .

The tile didn't suck in her whole body.

Twice . . .

It felt a little rubbery, and her foot bounced back a little.

Thrice.

"AAAAAH!"

She screamed because this time she *did* think she was getting sucked in, but it was just that the tile slid away so fast she almost fell. She popped open her eyes, quickly adjusted, and pulled herself back to the edge. She peered down to look inside, but all she could see was a simple gray tube. It went down about six feet and looked narrow, like a closed-top waterslide.

Gabby wasn't normally claustrophobic, but the Holobooth seemed like seriously close quarters for one person, never mind two.

"You really think the game will be better in there?" Gabby asked.

"Yes!" Trymmy enthused. Then his eyes and mouth made a sudden O. "One second."

He flashed out his finger and toe claws, then scrambled halfway up the wall until he could duck into one of the tunnels. Gabby heard the sound of rummaging, then a moment later he reappeared brandishing two backpacks. One was large, vinyl, and white with coffee-stained blotches; the other was a soft blue denim about the size of Gabby's own knapsack.

"Jet packs—so we can fly!" Trymmy declared. He slung the white one over his shoulders, draped the blue one around his neck, and scrambled back down the wall. Once he hopped down next to Gabby and retracted his claws, he handed her the blue pack. Though Gabby was dubious about wearing anything that would take up more space in the little tube, she said thanks and shrugged it on.

"You first," Trymmy said.

With trepidation, Gabby took a deep breath and sat at the edge of the round hole. Her feet dangled in. It really did look awfully narrow inside. Still, if this would make Trymmy happy . . .

Gabby squeezed her eyes shut, pushed off from the ledge, and stretched for the floor with her feet. She landed sooner than she'd imagined, and when she opened her eyes, she saw

nothing but gray walls, so near they closed her in. Things got even tighter a moment later when Trymmy slid in next to her. Gabby tried to push farther against the wall, but the backpack took up precious inches of space. Trymmy was crushed against her.

Gabby's whole body broke out in sweat. This was *not* a good idea. She thought she'd figured Trymmy out, but this had to be some kind of babysitter practical joke. How could they possibly play a game in here?

Trymmy grinned up at her. "Ready?"

Before Gabby could answer, Trymmy pressed an unseen button, and the tile hatch slid shut.

They were in complete darkness. Gabby couldn't breathe.

"Trymmy . . . ?" Gabby warbled.

"START THE GAME!" Trymmy hollered.

Gabby screamed as a booming sound filled her ears. She felt the sweet relief of space opening up around her, followed by terror as she swung back and up, as if a hook had curled into her spine and yanked her hard. Sparkling lights attacked her eyes, and she closed them, unwilling to see what they might reveal.

"GABBY!" Trymmy's voice somehow sliced through both her fear and the strange booming noise. "Open your eyes! We have to start!"

Gabby obeyed. She screamed again, but this time with

unbelievable delight. Trymmy was *flying*! The white vinyl backpack was a *real* jet pack, just like Trymmy had said! And the booming noise? Gabby realized it was *her own* jet pack! She was flying, too! And the vast world of sparkling lights all around her were stars twinkling through space.

Gabby tilted a little to her right and the jet pack swooshed her gently in that direction. She looked up . . . and *soared*. She tucked her chin to her chest and balled up her knees and squealed as she turned in an accidental somersault that kept the stars spinning even after her body had stopped.

"Trymmy, this is *amazing*!" Gabby cried. "How is this happening?"

"It's a Holobooth," Trymmy said as if it were the most obvious thing in the world. "It knows what I want to do and makes it happen. Now come on, let's play!"

For a second, Gabby had no idea what he meant. They were soaring through space on jet packs—what else could they possibly have to do? Then she noticed Trymmy's clenched fist and remembered the marbles. She plucked one randomly from the front pocket of her jeans where she'd stuffed them and held it out in her fist. She was about to count, but she didn't even open her mouth before a giant 3-D number three appeared in the air between her and Trymmy. The number changed, counting down, as a deeply resonant male voice boomed, "Three . . . two . . . one . . . go!"

Trymmy opened his hand. For the briefest second, Gabby saw a black-and-white marble in his palm, which immediately transformed into a giant blast of whistling wind. At the same time, Gabby opened her own hand. She didn't have the chance to look down and see what it was, but it had to be blue because a massive rush of water exploded out of Gabby's palm and moved in a giant wave toward Trymmy. When the wave collided with the wind, it dispersed into tiny droplets that sprayed over Gabby in a fine mist.

"Trymmy one, Gabby zero," the resonant voice declared. "Prepare for Round Two."

Gabby was breathless. Never in her wildest dreams could she have imagined this. She barely had a chance to take in what had just happened before the voice started counting down numbers and Gabby had to dig into her pocket once again.

"Three . . . two . . . one . . . go!"

Gabby and Trymmy opened their hands. The heat from a massive fireball seared Gabby's face as it flew toward her, but a second later it was doused by another tsunami wave from Gabby. Gabby heard the sizzle and felt the sudden humidity as the water evaporated away.

The game was the greatest experience of Gabby's life. It wasn't just the flying and the powers, either. It was Trymmy. *He* was so into it, whooping and hollering with each win, zooming through space to give Gabby a good-sport high five with each loss. Since the whole game came from his imagination, the powers changed constantly. Water could come in a wave, a geyser, or even a water creature who swallowed its opponent's fire in its gaping maw.

They played until Trymmy was hungry, then went up and grabbed some peanut butter sandwiches. Gabby's heart ached when she noticed Trymmy try to hide his face, as if Gabby might be disgusted watching him eat. She wondered if he had trouble with kids at school. They'd have no idea he was a Troll. They'd just think he was a very different-looking kid. A kid whose nose was so flat, he had to chew with his mouth open if he wanted to breathe. A kid whose nose *tip* hung so low over his lips that it got covered with food, and Trymmy had to lick it clean between bites. A kid whose longer, more dangly moles occasionally slipped between his lips as he chewed and had to be pooked back out again.

"I hope you're not totally grossed out," Gabby said as she leaned toward him conspiratorially.

"What do you mean?" Trymmy muttered, still bent over his elbow as he chewed.

Gabby sighed. "I probably need braces, 'cause I have this space between a couple of my back lower teeth. Every time I eat, something gets stuck there, and I hate feeling it there, so I end up making all these weird, gross faces until I get it out."

Trymmy peeked up from his arm. "Yeah?"

"People don't like to be around it much. You should see my fifth-grade class picture. I look like a cow."

She wasn't lying, and Trymmy seemed to sense it. He smiled, and didn't even lower his head back down when he licked a blob of peanut butter from the tip of his nose.

They went back into the Holobooth after dinner to continue their marble game. Gabby loved it even more now that she knew what to expect. She didn't think once about the time, or when Allynces and Feltrymm might come back, until all of a sudden gravity pulled hard on Gabby's body and she slammed back to her feet. Once again she was squished against Trymmy in a tiny gray tube.

"There you are!" Allynces wailed, and Gabby looked up to see the woman's angry face filling the circle above them. "I told Gabby to hide you down here in case of emergency! I thought something horrible had happened!"

Gabby flushed. "I'm so sorry. It's my fault. I didn't know we couldn't use the Holobooth to play."

"Of course Trymmy can use it to play, that's what it's for," Allynces snapped. "I just don't like that you were *both* down there. I thought the worst."

"I'm so, so sorry." Gabby blushed harder.

Trymmy didn't seem bothered. He climbed out of the Holobooth and hugged his mom hello. They were still embracing when Gabby emerged.

"You're so cuddly this evening, Trymmy," Allynces cooed, hugging him close. "Thank you."

Trymmy turned his head and winked. Warm happiness filled Gabby's chest. He'd given his mom the hug to distract her so she wouldn't stay mad at Gabby.

"Your service is complete, Gabby," Allynces said. "Feltrymm is in the garage. He'll take you home now."

Gabby stuck out her hand. "I just want to thank you so much for entrusting me with Trymmy. He's a great kid, and I hope I get the chance to—"

"Now," Allynces emphasized.

"Right," Gabby said. She started to shrug out of the denim backpack, but Trymmy stopped her.

"Keep it on," he said. "We can play more in the car." Then he turned to Allynces. "I can go with Dad to take her home, right?"

Allynces pursed her lips, but the long hug clearly had her in a good mood.

"Fine," she said, "but you're both in the back."

"Great!" Trymmy chirped. He spun excitedly to Gabby. "Can I grab your stuff?"

Gabby smiled. This happened a lot at the end of a job. The kids felt bad the playdate was ending and they went out of their way to do incredibly nice things for her. She always thought it was really sweet.

"Sure," she said. "That would be great. Thanks."

Gabby watched as Trymmy gathered her things, then ran back to her.

"Let's go!" he cried, and Gabby followed him down a tunnel to a surprisingly ordinary garage and car. They piled into the backseat, and Gabby waited for a ride similar to the one she took in Edwina's limousine. The clock on the dashboard said seven forty-five, and while she had no idea how far from home she was, she assumed it was far enough that only another wild trip would get her back by eight.

She was wrong. As she and Trymmy played the non-Holobooth version of Secret Mega Orbs, Gabby noticed the ride felt completely normal. They might not have even been speeding. It was too dark to see much outside the windows, but then, out of the corner of her eye, Gabby thought she saw the familiar neon window-sign of Bottle Rockets, her favorite candy store. The place was in the Square, a shopping area not too far from home. Was Trymmy's house really that close to hers? Gabby barely trusted her own eyes, until they passed another sign that Gabby would never mistake for anything else, since she saw it every single day.

"That's Brensville Middle School!" she cried. "I go there!"

"Really?" Trymmy said. "I go to Lion's Gate Academy."

This shocked Gabby. "Seriously? I babysit for kids there. I'm there a *lot*. How have I never seen you?"

Trymmy shrugged. He was more interested in the game. "Water beats fire. Your point. Let's play again."

"I can't believe you live close to me," Gabby said as she chose a marble for the next round. "What's your actual address?"

"Don't answer that, Trymmy," Feltrymm's voice sliced from up front. He glared at Gabby through the rearview mirror. "It's information we keep confidential."

Gabby felt hot with shame. No matter how impossibly otherworldly her evening with Trymmy had been, hanging out with him seemed so normal that she forgot this was anything other than a regular ride home. But no. Trymmy and his family were aliens. Aliens with giant stolen artifacts from history all over their property. They would *not* want anyone but the most trusted members of A.L.I.E.N. to know where they lived.

Gabby and Trymmy went back to the game, but all too soon the car pulled up to the curb in front of Gabby's house. "We're here!" Feltrymm said. "Time to get out!"

"I guess you'll need these," Trymmy said, holding out his three marbles.

"Keep them," Gabby said. "That way we can play again next time."

"Didn't you hear me say 'out'?" Feltrymm asked. "Out, out, out!"

"Yes, sir," Gabby said hurriedly, then turned to Trymmy.

"Guess I better take off my jet pack." She shrugged out of the blue denim backpack and reached for her own purple knapsack, but Trymmy stopped her.

"Can I help?" he asked.

His eyes looked wide open and melancholy. She wondered if he was thinking the same thing she was—that there was no way of knowing if she'd ever get the chance to babysit for him again. She smiled. "Of course."

"Turn around, please," Trymmy said.

Gabby did, and Trymmy held out first her jacket and then her knapsack, helping her put them on in true gentlemanly fashion.

"Do I need to explain the definition of the word 'out'?" Feltrymm groused.

"Sorry!"

Gabby quickly slipped from the backseat, but she barely made it out before Feltrymm screeched away, the taillights on his car speeding through her darkened development, then turning out of sight.

Already, Gabby missed Trymmy. If she didn't get to sit for him again, maybe she'd at least run into him the next time she had to meet a kid at Lion's Gate. That would be coincidence, so it wouldn't be the same as breaking Edwina's no-contact-outside-of-official-sitting-jobs rule.

Walking up her lawn, Gabby realized her knapsack felt a

little strange. As a rule, it weighed enough that it sunk down her back a little, but now it sat high on her shoulder blades. Maybe Trymmy had played with the straps. She swung it off to take a look . . .

. . . and realized it wasn't her purple knapsack at all.

It was the denim backpack. Gabby's jet pack. When she'd had it on just a few moments ago, it had been empty. Now there was something inside. Something heavy enough to make the weight feel *similar* to her purple knapsack, but not quite the same.

Gabby unzipped the pack. Inside was a plush Good Luck Troll doll—the kind with the wild hair and naked butt, like she'd mentioned earlier to Edwina. This particular doll was about a foot tall, with bright purple hair, a happy smile, and a butt that wasn't naked. In fact it wore jeans and a white T-shirt, with one word scrawled in marker across the shirt.

"GOTCHA!"

Gabby couldn't believe it. Edwina had warned her, but she'd let it happen anyway. She hadn't blinked an eye when Trymmy had asked "Can I grab your stuff?" She'd thought he was being sweet.

But no. He'd been doing what Trolls always do. He'd been stealing. And now he had Gabby's purple knapsack.

chapter SIX

This was bad.

Gabby *needed* her knapsack. She couldn't not have it. Her keys, her wallet, her babysitting tricks, her history book . . . they were *all* in the knapsack. Her *thumb drive* was in the knapsack, with the history paper that was due tomorrow!

Gabby raced down the street and screamed at the top of her lungs. "TRYMMY! FELTRYMM!"

But the car was long gone, and so was her backpack. All Gabby saw was a woman with a long gray braid down her back, who was walking her equally gray standard poodle along the sidewalk. The woman wasn't one of Gabby's neighbors, and clearly didn't care for Gabby's outburst. Her green eyes flashed a wicked glare in Gabby's direction, then she led her dog pointedly across the street. Gabby wondered if she should follow them and try to explain, but then she heard a garage door rumble open.

"Gabby?"

It was Alice's voice, and Gabby turned to see her mom pad out their open garage door and down their driveway. As she walked, Alice cinched a red puffy robe more tightly over her pajama bottoms and sweatshirt. "I thought I heard you shouting. Is everything okay?"

"It's fine, Mom!" Gabby called. She quickly trotted back to her house and plucked up the denim backpack she'd dropped on the lawn, then joined Alice next to their car. "I was . . . just yelling good-bye to Zee. Sorry if I was loud."

Alice threw a wiry arm around Gabby's shoulders and pulled her close. "I'm thrilled for the distraction," she admitted. "Let's get you inside."

The garage was packed floor to ceiling with years of memories, regretted purchases, and outgrown clothes and furniture. A single clear path ran from one end to the other, while the rest of the garage could only be accessed through a perilous network of antlike trails that Alice swore let her reach every single item should she be motivated enough to

excavate. As the two of them walked toward the inside door, Gabby noticed a large, ragged, and very familiar cardboard box. It was half-full of clothes, stuffed animals, and toys—things Gabby recognized from when she and Carmen were little.

"You're filling the box?" Gabby asked. "I thought you already did this month."

It had been Alice's New Year's resolution to slowly start tackling their garage by filling one large cardboard box a month, then donating the contents to charity. She'd diligently kept to the schedule, even though it hadn't made a dent.

"Getting a jump on next," Alice said, "but I mentioned it to Carmen and she got very worried about Mr. Octopants. I didn't even think she *remembered* Mr. Octopants."

Gabby snorted. Just a little. Alice smiled.

"I know, I know," Alice admitted, "your sister remembers everything. I'm just lucky she brought it up before I finished loading and donated it all." She reached into the cardboard box and pulled out a threadbare stuffed octopus wearing an eight-legged pair of khaki pants. "Packed and ready to go. Can you imagine?"

"Yes," Gabby answered, and both she and Alice shuddered as they pictured Carmen's horror. As they went inside together, Alice held Mr. Octopants at arms' length in front of them, so he could lead the way into the kitchen.

“See? Safe and sound. And look who else I found!” Alice shifted her arms in a flourish to showcase her eldest daughter.

“Gabby was in the giveaway box, too?” Carmen asked. For a girl who was desperately worried about her much-loved stuffie, she barely lifted her head to take in Mr. Octopants and her sister.

“You wish,” Gabby shot back.

Carmen was already dressed for bed in a long flannel nightgown and had her favorite dessert arrayed in front of her: parallel rows of blueberries, strawberries, and blackberries, served with a side bowl of whipped cream. The berries were to be eaten one at a time, in the proper order of strawberries, then blueberries, then blackberries, and only after receiving a two-second dip in the whipped cream bowl.

“She wishes no such thing,” Alice said as she placed Mr. Octopants on the chair next to Carmen, then breezed over to the refrigerator. “Berries for you, Gabby? I also have chocolate mousse.”

“Mousse, please,” Gabby said.

Carmen was staring at her.

“What?”

“Where’s your knapsack?” Carmen asked. “That one’s blue.”

Gabby froze. She’d been so involved with Mom and Carmen, she wasn’t even thinking about her knapsack.

“She’s right,” Alice said, frowning. “What happened? You never leave your knapsack anywhere.”

“It’s . . . um . . . it’s just with Zee,” Gabby stammered. “She spilled robot oil all over it, so she gave me this one to use while she cleans it up.”

“Robot oil?” Carmen repeated skeptically.

Gabby was sweating. She pulled off the blue backpack and her jacket. “Something like that. Whatever it was, it spilled.”

Peeling off a layer of her clothing did nothing to make Gabby more comfortable. Now her knapsack was back on her mind, and she had no idea if she’d ever see it again.

Then she remembered what Edwina had told her. Trolls had to give riddles to humans from whom they stole. If the human answered the riddle correctly, they’d get their item back.

But how would Trymmy get her a riddle?

Gabby needed to think this out. She was also suddenly desperate to get to her computer. She hoped like crazy she’d saved a copy of her history report onto her hard drive, but she was notoriously bad about that. Still, maybe she’d been more diligent this time. . . .

“Actually, I’m a little tired,” she told Alice. “I think I’m going to skip dessert and crawl into bed.”

“You should walk,” Carmen advised. “Better for your knees.”

Gabby scanned her sister’s stony face for evidence that

Carmen was joking. There wasn't any, but that didn't mean much.

"I'll do that," Gabby said. "Thanks, Car."

"Mmmm, I don't think so," Alice said. "You won't want to miss this." She placed a bowl in front of Gabby on the table. "I used dark chocolate. I don't want to brag, but the last time I served this, the host gave me a standing ovation. And this will only be here until I take it to tomorrow's luncheon, so believe me, now's the time."

The little glass bowl held a gorgeously swirled mound of rich chocolaty goodness, covered with a perfect dollop of whipped cream and dark chocolate shavings. Gabby may have been worried, but she wasn't nuts. And if she *hadn't* saved a copy of her history report, she was doomed. She'd never be able to re-create the whole thing by tomorrow. Better to enjoy her ignorance while she still could. As for the riddle, Gabby figured Trymmy could only send it to her via Edwina, and the fastest way for Edwina to get it to Gabby was by text. With that in mind, she set her phone screen-up next to her dessert, then sat and scooped a giant spoonful of mousse into her mouth.

She was just digging into her third deliriously thick and gorgeous bite when the doorbell rang.

Gabby froze. Could it be Trymmy with her riddle? She wanted to jump up and see, but Alice was already tightening her robe and striding around the corner to check the peephole.

"Madison Murray?" Alice called a second later.

Gabby choked on her mousse. Then she heard her mother inexplicably opening the door.

"Hi, Mrs. Duran," Madison's voice chirped. "Sorry I'm here so late. Is Gabby available?"

No, Gabby willed her mom to answer. *No, no, no.*

"She's in here eating chocolate mousse!" Carmen called. She smiled impishly for just a second, then turned back to study her berries intently as Madison flounced in.

It was the end of the day, but Madison's tailored blouse and skirt looked perfectly clean and ironed, and her blond hair draped to her shoulders in fresh-blown waves. Even the pink shopping bag she set down next to her looked completely pristine, with crisp folds at every edge.

"Hi, Madison." Gabby forced a smile.

"You have chocolate in your teeth," Madison replied.

Of course she did. Gabby ducked her head and worked her tongue over the entire inside of her mouth.

"Would you like some chocolate mousse, Madison?" Alice asked.

"I can't," Madison said sweetly. "I care about my complexion."

Alice let the insult slide. "And how are things going with H.O.O.T.? It's just two days away, right?"

Madison seemed to glow at the mention of her big event. "Yes! Actually, that's why I'm here. I've decided to honor Gabby with the most important role of the entire auction."

She leaned so close that Gabby could smell whatever lavender lotion or detergent clung to her clothes and skin. "Gabby Duran, you get to be the official H.O.O.T. mascot . . . Hooty the H.O.O.T. Owl!"

With a flourish, Madison reached into the bag and pulled out a giant monstrosity of a brown, fuzzy, person-shaped rug. The arms ended in nappy mittens; the belly had a large circle of what might have been white once, but was now a dingy gray with blotches of uncertain origin; the ankles emptied into extra-large flat plastic flippers.

The chocolate mousse turned to mud in Gabby's stomach.

"I'm supposed to wear that?!" she spluttered. "That's—"

"So precious!" Alice finished.

Gabby wheeled to her mom, positive Alice had to be joking. But no, her mom's face was all round and eager, like she was staring at a litter of kittens instead of a decrepit sheath of matted fur.

"I know, right?" Madison enthused. "And wait until you see the best part!"

Before Gabby could protest, Madison ducked around the back of Gabby's chair and plopped something onto Gabby's head. Gabby was instantly plummeted into a disorienting semidarkness in which she nearly passed out from the mixed scents of mothballs and sweat.

"Wow. You must really hate Gabby." Carmen's muffled voice reached Gabby through the layers of fabric and must.

"Carmen, don't be ridiculous. It's adorable!" Alice crowed.

"I'm wearing an owl head, aren't I," Gabby deadpanned.

"It's so sweet," Alice cooed. "Gabby, you have to see it."

Gabby's mom pulled out her chair, then guided her to the hallway mirror.

"Let me know when you can see," Alice said.

Gabby felt the head tilt and swirl on her shoulders until finally two ovals of mesh netting lined up with her own eyes. Right away, she wished she were back in total blackness. The owl head was the same poofy brown as the body, but with fuzzy white fringes outlining massive goo-goo eyes that must have shifted over the costume's long life because one was cross-eyed and the other stared up and to the left. Add that to the overbite on the bright yellow beak, and the owl looked like it had slammed into one too many trees.

"Don't you love it?" Alice asked. "Now put on the body. I want to see it all together."

"But then you won't be surprised when you see it all Tuesday," Gabby said. "Wouldn't want to ruin that great moment."

Gabby pulled off the head and gulped in fresh air. In the

mirror she saw her face was frighteningly red and sweaty, and her curls stuck out in every direction, as if they were running away to enjoy their newfound freedom.

"Oh good," Madison said. "I'm glad it comes off easily. That way you can unmask when the auction's over so everyone knows how amazing you were running around and dancing and getting the crowd all crazy."

Or more accurately, so everyone could see Gabby look like a giant electrocuted lobster. "Thanks, Madison," Gabby said. "You really thought of everything."

"Speaking of which . . . Mrs. Duran, can I talk to Gabby privately for a second?"

"Of course. Why don't you girls go up to Gabby's room?"

Gabby could think of at least a million reasons why she and Madison shouldn't go up to her room, but she didn't feel like she could say no, so she led her worst enemy upstairs.

"Ew, seriously?" Madison screeched as Gabby opened the door and she saw the wall-to-wall laundry. "How do you live like this?"

Gabby knew she shouldn't care what Madison thought of her mess, but seeing it through Madison's eyes still made her shrink inside. "I was planning to clean it tomorrow," she lied.

"I would hope so." Madison tiptoed along the room's lone strip of visible carpet until she stood in front of Gabby's dresser. Wincing, she ran a finger along its edge, inspected her fingertip for dust, then leaned gingerly against what she clearly saw as an island of cleanliness in a churning ocean of sewage.

Gabby was losing patience. "So, is what you want more or less humiliating than having me run around in a sweaty, disgusting owl suit?"

Madison stood taller against the dresser. "Gabby, I told you—being Hooty is an *honor*. I gave you the part to be nice to you. I want us to be friends."

Gabby searched Madison's eyes for sarcasm and was shocked she couldn't find it. Had Madison actually turned some kind of corner? Was the nasty owl suit her misguided way of holding out an olive branch? Had Gabby's years and years of trying to win her over finally worked?

"Wow, Madison," Gabby said, moved. "That's really great. I always thought we should be—"

"And friends do things for one another, right?" Madison asked.

Inwardly, Gabby slapped herself for falling into Madison's trap. Of course the girl had an ulterior motive.

"What do you want, Madison?"

Madison took a deep breath. Her cheeks grew red, and she looked down at the floor. "I'm in big trouble," she said softly. "I need your help."

Gabby was confused. Once again, Madison looked and

sounded sincere. Was she really turning to Gabby for help?

"What kind of trouble?" she asked.

"It's about H.O.O.T.," Madison admitted. "When I decided to do an auction, Maestro Jenkins didn't think it was a good idea. He said it would be too hard to make the ten thousand dollars we needed. He told me to do something that worked before, like a big carnival, or a bake sale . . ."

"Or the five-K, like last year!" Gabby lit up thinking about it. "That was so fun, remember? Everyone paid to enter, then they bought T-shirts, and we had that raffle at the finish line party, and—"

"Not helping," Madison said.

"Sorry," Gabby said. "But the auction will be great. You've been promoting it like crazy, and you're doing that live streaming thing. Plus, you have that big secret item, right? I mean, that'll be huge."

"It would be," Madison said, "if I had it."

"You don't?"

"I *did*," she clarified, meeting Gabby's eyes for just a second before looking away again. "I mean, I *thought* I did. One of my mom's sorority sisters manages Sukie Elliston. Sukie's on tour, and Mom thought her friend could put together this whole package: concert tickets, backstage pass, hanging out with Sukie. It would have been huge."

"It would have been amazing!" Gabby gushed.

"Sukie Elliston's like the most popular singer *ever*. And did you see that superhero movie she did over the summer? Satchel and I saw it like six times—in the theater!"

Gabby realized Madison's face had paled, and she was staring at Gabby with her lips pursed into a straight, bloodless line. Gabby toned down her enthusiasm and folded her hands together.

"Right," she said. "Not helping again. So what happened to the package?"

"Turns out Mom was wrong. Her friend can't do any of that. Or she *can*, but we found out tonight she *won't*. She's just donating a signed concert poster."

Gabby felt herself deflate at the letdown, but she tried not to let it show. "Okay, but that's something, right?"

"It's not enough," Madison said. "Nothing I have is enough. Not to get to ten thousand dollars. And that means we won't go to MusicFest. Unless some *other* member of the Brensville Middle School Orchestra . . ."

Madison pulled away from her perch and stepped toward Gabby, not even paying attention to the laundry on the floor.

". . . someone who knows *lots* of celebrities . . ."

She moved even closer to where Gabby sat on her bed. Gabby felt like she was being stalked.

". . . and someone who's my very-super-special-good friend . . ."

Madison plopped next to Gabby on the bed and grinned in her face. The grin looked oddly robotic and maniacal. Gabby reared back to get away from it.

". . . unless *that* person calls their celebrity connections right now and gets us a donation as amazing as the Sukie Elliston thing. Then I can announce it just like I'd planned—giving you credit, of course—and we'll go down in history as the team who made the most money for MusicFest ever."

Staring into Madison's eerily intense smile, Gabby considered it. She *did* have celebrities on her babysitting client list. Superstar actors even, like Adam Dent and Sierra Bonita. And she was close enough to them that if she asked, they probably would donate something that fell into the amazing category. Maybe even so amazing that Madison would get huge bids from all over the world with her live streaming auction, and the final price could fund MusicFest not just for this year, but for Gabby's entire middle school career. Gabby could imagine how incredible it would feel, swooping in to save the day. She'd be a hero. The whole orchestra would love her. Maestro Jenkins would love her. Madison would probably want to be her best friend for real.

But Gabby could also imagine how she'd feel *after* the auction, when people she barely knew buffeted her for information about the Bonita-Dents' personal lives. Or asked her to

try and get more out of them for other events. Or tried to follow her around so maybe they could meet the actors one day.

There was a reason Gabby kept her client list to herself. She liked the people who hired her for who they were, not their celebrity, and she respected their privacy. Even if it was for a good cause, she didn't want to take advantage.

Gabby reached up and twirled a curl around her finger. "What makes you think I know celebrities?"

"Please, Gabby. We've all seen you get picked up by limousines. And the helicopter on the soccer field?"

Oops, Gabby thought, popping the curl in her mouth. That hadn't exactly been inconspicuous. But when the president of the United States needs a babysitter, sometimes she needs that babysitter *now*.

"Okay, I might know a few celebrities," Gabby admitted. "But I can't ask them for things. I'm sorry. I can help you in other ways though. Like, maybe if we added something to the auction, like a car wash or a face painting booth or—"

"None of that will work, Gabby!" Madison snapped. "Now here's the deal. No one knows I had a celebrity connection, but everyone believes you do. Either you help me, or I'll say *you* were the one who was supposed to deliver the Special Can't-Miss Surprise and you backed out."

"But that's a lie!"

"No one else will know that. And when we don't earn

enough for MusicFest, and we don't get to go for the first time *ever*, everyone will blame *you.* Not me, *you.* And you know what? You'll deserve it, because you're being totally selfish. You're supposed to *care* about orchestra, and you don't. You just care about keeping your special little celebrities to your special little self. So you think about that, Gabby Duran, and if you change your mind, call me. If not . . ."

Madison didn't even bother finishing the threat. She tried to flounce out of the room, but a pair of Gabby's underwear caught on her shoe. She roared in frustration as she kicked it away. "And clean your room!"

This time she made it out. Gabby heard her pound down the steps and out the door.

Gabby flopped back onto her bed. The knapsack, the owl costume, Madison . . . It was too much. And it was all completely unfair! She'd been nice to Trymmy, and she'd always tried to be nice to Madison, but they still went out of their way to wreck her life. What she really wanted to do was dive into a vat of her mom's dark chocolate mousse and forget everything else.

"Hey."

Alice's voice came from the bedroom door. Gabby grunted something that may or may not have sounded like a reply. She felt the pressure of her mom sitting down on the bed.

"I owe you an apology," Alice said.

“For not bringing me more chocolate mousse?” Gabby asked.

“Nope,” Alice said, “because *that* I actually did.”

Gabby bolted upright. Sure enough, her mom held a bowl of dark chocolate heaven. Gabby grabbed it and took a bite. Already she felt a million times better.

“I owe you an apology for listening in,” Alice continued. “I heard what Madison said, and I want to help. I can call her mother and—”

“Don’t, please,” Gabby muttered between bites. “You know her mom. She’ll just stick up for whatever Madison says, even if it’s a lie.”

Alice opened her mouth to object, but then she closed it again with a sigh. “You’re right. Can I have a bite?”

Gabby handed Alice the spoon and her mom skimmed it over the dessert, catching an even ratio of whipped cream and mousse.

“*Am* I being selfish?” Gabby asked. “I mean, I *could* make a call and get something amazing for the auction.”

“You could,” Alice said. She pointed the spoon at Gabby. “And how would that make you feel?”

“Awful,” Gabby said, snatching the spoon so she could grab some more mousse. “Like I was betraying people I care about.”

Alice’s mouth curled up in a half-smile. “Then . . .”

"But maybe the celebrities wouldn't feel that way!" Gabby interjected. "Maybe Adam and Sierra would *want* to help!"

"I didn't ask how they would feel," Alice said. "I asked how *you* would feel. And if you feel like you'd be breaking a trust, you shouldn't do it. And you certainly shouldn't compromise your beliefs because of some threat by an over-indulged little snoot."

Gabby laughed. "That's the closest I've ever heard you come to saying something mean about anyone."

"Well she deserved it," Alice said. She leaned over and kissed Gabby on top of her head. "You're doing the right thing, baby. And don't worry. I have a feeling it'll all work out."

Gabby couldn't fathom how that could possibly be true, but it sounded good, so for the moment she decided to believe it. After her mom left, Gabby checked her phone, but there was nothing from Edwina, no riddle.

Then she did what she'd dreaded most. She rolled out of bed and moved slowly to her desk. She tapped her computer keyboard to wake up the machine, then murmured out loud, begging the Gabby of the past two months to have been way more responsible and diligent than she remembered her being.

"Please, Gabby," she implored herself as she clicked through files. "Please tell me you saved the history report."

Gabby laughed triumphantly as she saw a copy of the file. She clicked it open . . .

. . . and her whole being sunk as she stared at a bullet-point outline on the screen.

She checked the date on the file and realized it was a month old. Everything she'd done in the past month was *only* on the thumb drive, and the thumb drive was on her keychain, in her knapsack, somewhere with Trymmy.

Gabby buried her head in her hands and gripped her hair. She was in bigger trouble than she'd ever been in her life, and that included being chased by an evil G.E.T.O.U.T. agent who wanted to kill her. The report was due tomorrow, at the beginning of sixth period history class. Ms. McKay had said over and over again that there'd be no extensions. Even if you were home sick, you had to e-mail it in on time. There was no way Gabby could re-create a month's work by then, even if she stayed up all night and skipped every class until history. If she didn't get her thumb drive back, she'd get a zero on a paper that was thirty percent of her grade. She could go from a B to a D. And if her grade fell that low, Alice would pull her out of orchestra. She wouldn't let Gabby babysit. She'd have to give up *everything*.

The room was getting swimmy. Gabby was hyperventilating. She tucked her head between her knees like she'd seen in movies, but it only made her dizzier.

She needed to talk to someone. It was late, but she could call Zee and she would answer. Zee's cousin Kat was in

England for a semester abroad and liked to call Zee at weird times, so Zee always kept her phone on and close by, even at night.

Gabby had already started dialing when she got a better idea. What she *really* needed was Trymmy's riddle. If she had that, she could solve it and get her knapsack back, ideally before sixth period. How could she prod Trymmy to get her the riddle right away?

Edwina.

Edwina had said that if Gabby saw anyone strange following her, she should take a picture and Edwina would somehow see it. Following that logic, Gabby grabbed a piece of notebook paper and scrawled out a message: "TRYMMY TOOK MY KNAPSACK. NEED RIDDLE A.S.A.P. PLEASE!" She snapped a picture, then stared at her phone for ten minutes, willing it to respond. When it didn't, she decided to go to bed but brought her phone with her. If Edwina did reply, Gabby didn't want to miss it. She closed her eyes . . .

. . . and opened them when a duck quacked into her ear.

It wasn't a real duck, it was her e-mail alert.

Gabby grabbed the phone. It said it was five in the morning, and she had one new message.

The message was from TRYMMY01@trollnet.xqz.

The subject line? "YOUR RIDDLE."

chapter SEVEN

Despite Edwina's warning about not having contact with aliens outside babysitting, Gabby didn't hesitate to click the e-mail open. She desperately needed the riddle, and reading an e-mail couldn't possibly put Trymmy in any danger. Besides, how could Trymmy have gotten Gabby's address except from Edwina? That meant Edwina had to approve.

Gabby read the message. It said:

FOR GABBY DURAN
A RIDDLE IN TWO PARTS

I.

You'll find it in a kitchen, any old day.
Take away its blueness, and it'll be okay.
Pull off its tail, and it'll sound like a dove,
When it's good, it makes you things you love.

II.

Life is often a volume of grief,
I need your help to turn a leaf.
My spine is stiff,
And my body is pale,
But I'm always ready,
To tell a tale.

Bring me the object described in these rhymes,
And your knapsack will come back in record time.

She waited for an answer to spring into her head, but when nothing immediately came, she quickly forwarded the e-mail to Zee, then called to wake her up. It was too early for a call, but this was dire. As the phone rang, Gabby moved to her computer and pulled up the riddle there.

"Kat?" Zee mumbled sleepily.

"Sorry, Zee. It's Gabby."

"Gabs!" Instantly, Zee sounded completely awake. "Is

everything okay? Did you get me alien DNA?"

"No, but the alien probably got some of mine. Does DNA stick to knapsacks?"

"Is that a riddle? 'Cause it's way too early for riddles."

"I hope that's not true," Gabby said, then she told Zee everything. Before she had even finished the entire story, she heard Zee tapping on computer keys.

"Okay," Zee said. "I have it on my screen . . . I'm reading . . . I'm thinking . . ."

"Yeah, me too," Gabby said. Then she jumped in her chair and screamed so loud she was afraid she'd wake up her mom and Carmen. "Oh! I think I have it! I think I have the second part!"

"Hit me," Zee said.

"Okay, check it out," Gabby said. "'Life is often a volume of grief, I need your help to turn a leaf. My spine is stiff, and my body is pale, but I'm always ready, to tell a tale.' It's a book, right? It has to be. A *volume*, turning a *leaf*, the *spine*, *telling a tale* . . . and the pale body part is just that the pages are white so you can read the ink!"

"Yes!" Zee crowed. "Now let's look at the first part."

"Okay," Gabby said. "'You'll find it in a kitchen, any old day.' A blowtorch?"

"A *blowtorch*?"

"Yeah. For caramelizing the top of a crème brûlée."

"Okay, Gabs? Think about a *normal* person's kitchen, not a my-mom's-an-awesome-caterer kitchen."

"An anti-griddle?"

"I'm banning you from working on this line of the riddle," Zee said. "Let's look at the rest."

For a moment there was nothing but the sound of the two girls murmuring to themselves as they read the clue out loud.

"Oh! Oh! Yes! I have it!" Zee cried.

"You do?"

"Yeah, yeah! It's all about the third line: 'pull off its tail, and it'll sound like a dove.'"

"What animal sounds like a dove when you pull off its tail?" Gabby asked.

"No animal. The clue is saying you get the sound a dove makes when you pull off the tail of the *answer*—the last letter of the answer. So what sound does a dove make?"

"A dove coos," Gabby said.

"Right! So when you pull off the last letter of the answer, you'll get 'coo'—the sound a dove makes. Pull off its tail and it'll sound like a dove!"

Gabby jounced her knees up and down. They were so close. She could feel it. "Okay, so the answer has to be C-O-O-something." Her whole body electrified as she got it. "COOK! It has to be cook!"

"Totally! And it can go with the other clues. A cook is in

the kitchen, any old day; when a cook is good, it makes you things you love."

"And the blueness?" Gabby asked.

"Just figured that out. It's totally cool, and makes me want to meet your alien even more. Know what cobalt is?"

"It's a paint color, right?"

"A *blue* paint color," Zee affirmed. "But it's also an element on the periodic table, with the atomic symbol . . . wait for it . . . *CO*."

Gabby's eyes grew wide. "So if you take away the *blueness* from 'cook,' you take away the C-O . . ."

". . . and you're left with O-K. 'Take away its blueness, and it'll be okay!' Dude, is it bad that I'm kind of the teeniest bit psyched this kid took your knapsack and gave us this riddle?"

"Yes. Very bad," Gabby replied. "But at least we have the answer. The first part is 'cook,' and the second part is 'book,' so Trymmy needs a cookbook!"

"And whose mom is a caterer with like a zillion cookbooks?" Zee asked.

"Mine!" Gabby cheered. "Zee, this is perfect! Now I just have to do the 'bring me the object described in these rhymes' part. That's easy. Trymmy goes to Lion's Gate Academy. I'll grab a cookbook, ride my bike there, and get him before he starts class!"

"Wait," Zee said. "Didn't you say Edwina gave you the

no-go on seeing alien kids when you're not sitting them?"

"Yes, but she also told me I was the one who had to get my stuff back if it was taken," Gabby pointed out. "The riddle says bring him the object—I can't do that if I don't go see him, so that's got to be an exception, right?"

"Totally an exception," Zee agreed. "You're following the riddle instructions. That's what you're supposed to do."

"Exactly," Gabby affirmed. "And if I *don't* get the bag, and I get a zero on my paper, and my grade drops, and I can't babysit anymore, then I can't help A.L.I.E.N. at all."

"You're right," Zee said. "This is the call. We go to Lion's Gate."

"We?" Gabby echoed dubiously.

"*We,*" Zee maintained, "because I can get you there and back fast enough that you won't miss any classes."

"Seriously?" Gabby asked. Lion's Gate Academy wasn't exactly close to Brensville Middle School by bike. Gabby had already resigned herself to skipping her first few classes, but it would be amazing if she didn't have to. "How?"

"Just trust me," Zee said. "Grab a cookbook, ride your bike to our school, then meet me at the robotics shed as soon as humanly possible."

Whatever Zee had in mind, Gabby trusted it would be brilliant.

"Done," she said, then hung up and quickly scrambled

through a shower, getting dressed, and mussing some goo through her curls to tamp down the frizz factor. She tossed everything she'd need for the day into the blue denim bag, all the while rejoicing that she'd be swapping it out for her knapsack in no time at all.

With the house still quiet, she ducked downstairs to pick a cookbook for Trymmy. She figured she'd take whichever one looked the least familiar, since maybe that would be one Alice wouldn't miss. She readied her phone, too, so she could take a picture of whatever book she chose. That way she could order a new copy online and have a replacement before Alice knew it was gone.

Gabby had planned to beeline for the pantry, which doubled as a cookbook library, but then she saw the giant cardboard box on the kitchen table. It was the same one Gabby had seen in the garage last night, only now it was full. Alice must have been motivated to finish loading it after Gabby and Carmen went to bed. Gabby peered into it, just to make sure she didn't see any toys that Carmen might randomly freak out over one day if they were gone.

She didn't, but she did notice something on top of the pile of random odds and ends.

It was a book. The thing was greenish-colored, and very thick and old-looking. Gabby leaned over curiously to look at it more closely. She expected it to be a desperately boring

old textbook from her mother's college days, maybe calculus or accounting.

Instead, what she saw on the cover made her almost squeal out loud.

Joy of Cooking.

Gabby's insides danced. It was a cookbook! An old, faded cookbook at the very top of the giveaway pile, which meant Alice didn't want it anymore! Gabby hefted the book and hugged it to her chest—it was perfect!

A little too perfect. Keeping the book close, Gabby wheeled around in both directions. Was Edwina here? Had she put the book on top of the pile? It wasn't impossible. Even though she'd *said* A.L.I.E.N. wouldn't get involved if the Trolls stole anything from Gabby, was it that hard to believe she wanted to help?

It wasn't hard to believe at all, and the small knot of worry inside Gabby finally relaxed. Despite what she'd said to Zee, Gabby had still felt a little uneasy about violating Edwina's no-visits rule, but this was as clear an indication as Gabby could get that the woman approved.

Gabby saw no sign of Edwina, but she knew from experience that meant nothing.

"Thank you," she whispered to anyone who might be listening, then stuffed the cookbook into Trymmy's denim backpack and tiptoed up to her mom's room. Alice was fast

asleep, her always-wild hair splayed Medusa-like over her pillow. Gabby knelt down and leaned in close.

"Mom?"

She reached out and shook Alice's arm gently until Alice said something like, "Mmmphmmmblllbrrphllllt."

Gabby took that as a signal to keep going.

"Zee and I have those history papers due today, and we want to go over them together one last time," Gabby lied. She was getting way too good at lying, but she reminded herself that it wasn't a *complete* lie, and in general she only lied when absolutely necessary. "I'm going to ride my bike and meet her at school early. Is that okay?"

"Mbbblllggrrphhmmmbleeee."

"Mom?" Gabby shook Alice's arm again. She couldn't leave unless she was sure Alice understood her, or Alice would panic when she got up and Gabby wasn't there.

Now Alice opened her eyes. "Gabby?" she mumbled sleepily. "Hey, baby. Is everything okay?"

Gabby gave her the story again, and this time Alice nodded. "That's fine. Here, let me get you some breakfast."

She started to roll out of bed, but Gabby stopped her. "It's okay, I'll grab something with Zee. You can rest. The alarm won't go off for another twenty minutes."

Alice smiled. "Thanks, baby," she murmured. "Ride safe. Love you."

She plopped her head back on the pillow and instantly fell back to sleep. Just in case she woke up thinking their conversation was a dream, Gabby scrawled a quick note on the pad of paper on Alice's nightstand—the one where Alice wrote all the wild recipes she came up with as she slept. Then Gabby sidled out of the room, ran downstairs, grabbed her purple jacket, and sprinted to her bike. Luckily, the orchestra members were using all their practice periods to do things for H.O.O.T. There was no way Gabby could carry the backpack *and* her French horn on her bicycle.

Thinking about H.O.O.T. made Gabby a little nauseous, so she pumped her pedals even harder to push it out of her head. The sun was barely up and the frigid morning wind bit into her face, but she was riding so hard that the chill was a relief.

It wasn't long before she pulled her bike up to the robotics shed, which was the least shedlike structure Gabby had ever seen. It was an enormous brick building that, as Gabby understood it, was used generations ago for electives like home ec and shop. For years the school used it only for storage, but when Principal Tate took over the robotics club, he renovated the space and dedicated it to his team.

Was Zee already here? Had Gabby beaten her?

She reached out for the doorknob and nearly fell in as Zee whisked open the door. Her braids clung to her face in

sweaty strips, but she was grinning. "Perfect!" she said. "You got the book?"

Gabby shrugged off the blue backpack and tugged out the giant tome. Zee grimaced. "Wow. I'm bored just looking at it."

"I bet that's why my mom had it in the charity pile," Gabby said. "So how are we going to get to Lion's Gate?"

Zee grinned wider, then pushed the robotics shed door all the way open and had Gabby hold it so she could roll something out. The "something" looked like a surfboard, but with four sets of skateboard wheels and some kind of jet booster on the back.

"What *is* that?" Gabby asked.

"It's a surfboard, but with four sets of skateboard wheels and a jet booster on the back," Zee said.

Gabby cringed. "Tell me you don't expect me to ride that thing to Lion's Gate Academy."

"No way! You'd kill yourself!" Zee said.

"Good."

"*I'm* riding it," Zee said, "You're holding on tight." She ducked back inside the robotics shed and came out with her overstuffed camouflage duffel slung over her back and two helmets in her hands. She gave one helmet to Gabby and put the other on herself. When she spoke again, Gabby was only slightly surprised to find she could hear Zee perfectly through a helmet-to-helmet microphone system. It was the kind of detail only Zee would think of.

"Let me get on first," Zee said. "Then step on the back half, hold on to my waist, and bend your knees."

Gabby did as she was told. Zee had tried to teach her to ride a skateboard a thousand times in their years of friendship, but Gabby always toppled over the second both feet were off the ground. This board felt even wobblier than anything Zee had given her before. She tottered precariously, swaying back and forth. She tried to get a good hold on Zee's waist, but it was covered by the camouflage duffel. Gabby's arms could barely stretch around the bag.

"Just promise me you'll warn me before we start," Gabby said nervously. "It'll be worse if I'm sur—AAAAAAA!!!!!"

With no hint at all, Zee stomped her foot on a hidden button, and the engines jumped to life. Somehow Zee had rigged them not to make a sound, but they jolted the surfboard forward at what felt like light speed. Gabby's stomach lagged behind as the rest of her bounced over dirt and grass so quickly her feet flew into thin air. Only a little bit, but to Gabby it may as well have rocketed her into space. She curled her fingers tightly into Zee's duffel bag and tried to will her body to stay upright.

"Get low!" Zee cried through the intercom. "Like me! You'll fall if you stand straight up!"

Zee hunched lower, bending her knees and holding out her arms for balance. Gabby wouldn't hold out her arms for anything, but she forced herself into a knock-kneed squat.

"Are you sure this is a good idea?" Gabby asked through chattering teeth.

"I wasn't a second ago," Zee admitted. "I thought the board might fall apart as soon as it took off. But it's working! Cool, right? I'll get us to Lion's Gate in ten minutes."

Zee was a wheeled-vehicle expert. She knew every skate-able back road and path in the entire township. She used them all now, leaning her body to steer through brush, around stumps, and over rutted dirt trails. Gabby tried to close her eyes, but that only made her feel more unbalanced. Instead she focused on a small patch of camouflage like nothing else existed in the world.

Suddenly, a fierce jolt threw Gabby into the dirt in the middle of a thicket of bushes. Zee leaped off the board and crouched next to her.

"You okay, Gabs? I'm so sorry. I should have told you we were stopping."

But Gabby was too transfixed to care. The thicket where Zee had stopped reared up against a beautifully manicured field. Stone steps led from the field down to a lower court-yard, where basketball, handball, and tetherball courts shared open space with a playground, another field, and a sprawl of cabins. The cabins looked rustic from the outside, but Gabby had seen their insides and knew they held the finest in educational technology, plus a kaleidoscope of student art, projects, and writing samples.

Lion's Gate Academy.

Gabby and Zee had made even better time than they'd hoped. It was only seven thirty. The doors to the school didn't officially open until eight, when everyone arrived. Then there was a half hour of before-class playtime, during which Gabby could find Trymmy, hand him the cookbook, get her knapsack, then zoom back to Brensville ideally right on time for her first class of the day.

"Zee, you are a genius," Gabby proclaimed.

"'Very Superior' I'm told is the official classification," Zee said, "but I'll take it."

The two friends settled in the grass and waited. Gabby was too anxious to do anything but watch the field. Zee opened her camouflage duffel bag and spread out her robot parts to work on Wilbur.

Gabby whispered down the last seconds. "Three . . . two . . . one . . ."

At eight o'clock on the dot the fields and playgrounds burst to life with kids wearing the khakis, reds, and blues of the Lion's Gate Academy's uniform. Gabby strained her eyes

looking for Trymmy, but from her vantage point every kid looked alike.

"I'm going in," Gabby said. She sprang to her feet, stormed out of the thicket, and ran onto the giant field.

"Hey, Gabby!"

"Gabby Duran!"

"Hi, Gabbeeeee!!!"

Gabby had babysat a bunch of Lion's Gate kids. She returned every wave, smile, and torpedo-slam hug, but all the while her eyes searched wildly for Trymmy.

Then a deep, stern voice boomed, "Gabby? Is that you, soldier?"

It was Gareth, Lion's Gate's head playground monitor. Gabby often ended up chatting with him after class while whatever kid she was sitting hung out on the playground with friends.

"It is," Gabby replied, eyes still darting all around. "Hi, Gareth."

Gareth straightened into a salute. He had been a marine and still looked the part, with bulging muscles and close-cropped hair. He knew Gabby's dad had been in the military and was lost in the line of duty. Out of respect, he always treated Gabby like a fellow soldier, sometimes even an officer.

"At ease," Gabby said, returning his salute. "Hey, do you

know Trymmy? I left something at his place when I was babysitting him yesterday. I'm supposed to meet him and pick it up."

"Trymmy?" Gareth asked, scrunching up his face. "I didn't know he was one of yours. Strange little guy, that one. Don't you think?"

Gabby had always liked Gareth, so she was surprised by his words. Gareth worked with these kids. He was supposed to care about them. How could he call one of them strange? The word was Gabby's least favorite on the planet. It was what people loved to call Carmen when they didn't want to bother to go any deeper. She was "strange" because of her too-short bangs, or the precise way she ate her food, or her lack of comforting smiles in conversation.

"Strange how?" Gabby retorted, and Gareth must have heard the challenge in her voice because he stepped back and blushed.

"'Strange' wasn't really the right word. He's just . . . you know . . . unique."

Gabby raised an eyebrow. "Unique" was the same as "strange," and Gareth knew it.

"Look in the Lost and Found," Gareth finally muttered. "That's where he usually hangs."

"He hangs out in the Lost and Found?" Gabby gawped. "Alone?"

Gareth rubbed the back of his neck uncomfortably. "He seems to like it there."

Gabby shook her head and walked away. At Brensville, the Lost and Found was a smelly Dumpster behind the gym. At Lion's Gate, it had a whole building to itself—a shack that used to house the preschoolers before their new building opened. Inside it looked a lot like a very small department store, with uniform shirts, jackets, and pants—how did kids lose their pants?—dangling off hangers in racks. Shelving units showed off abandoned lunch boxes, notebooks, and even musical instruments, which was a crime against everything Gabby held dear. She looked up and down every aisle and found him in the last one. He was lying on the floor under a rack of blue and red uniform sweaters, reaching up his arms to bat at their hems and make them swing.

"Trymmy?" she asked.

"Gabby!" Trymmy bolted to a seated position, which made the sweater-bottoms hang low on his thick forehead like a hat. "I was hoping you'd come! You got my riddle?"

"Got it and solved it," Gabby said. She shrugged off the denim bag and pulled out the old green-covered volume. "A cookbook. Am I right?"

Trymmy spread his bulbous lips in a smile. "See for yourself." He nodded behind Gabby.

When she turned, her purple knapsack was right there,

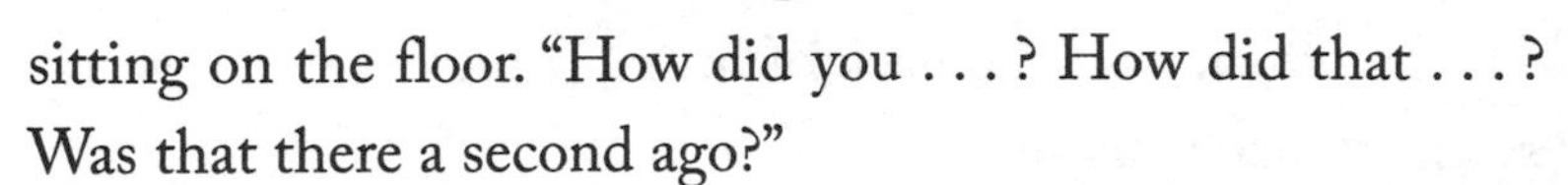

sitting on the floor. "How did you . . . ? How did that . . . ? Was that there a second ago?"

"Nope," Trymmy said. "That's just the way it works. The riddle gets answered and the item goes back where it belongs."

Gabby shoved the cookbook into Trymmy's arms, then snatched up her knapsack and hugged it close. "Thank you. I'm still mad at you for taking it, though."

Trymmy got to his feet, unintentionally burying his head in sweaters. "Don't be mad, please? You can't be mad. Stealing is what Trolls do. We can't help it. And you gave me permission. I asked if I could grab your stuff and you said yes."

"Yeah, but I didn't mean—" Gabby stopped herself, because she knew Trymmy was right. She sighed in defeat. "Okay, yeah, I kind of did."

"So you're not mad."

"No." Gabby scooched down on her knees so she could unzip her knapsack and reach inside. Trymmy dropped down next to her.

"Oh come on, you don't think I took anything, do you?" he asked. "I wouldn't do that!"

Gabby pulled out her keys, her purple thumb drive blissfully attached to the ring. She kissed it.

"I didn't think you took anything," she assured Trymmy. "I just had to make sure this was here." She quickly put

her keys back, added in the few items she'd had in the blue backpack—his Good Luck Troll included—then shouldered her knapsack and stood.

"Thanks for the riddle, Trymmy. I hope we get to play again sometime."

"Like now!" Trymmy scrambled back to his feet so quickly that all his bigger moles boinged up and down. "Classes don't start for a while. I have my marbles."

He dug into his pocket and pulled out the three marbles Gabby had given him the night before. Gabby's heart melted a little.

"You keep them with you?" she asked.

Gabby thought she could detect the slightest blush behind his sea of moles, but he looked away before she could really tell. "Same pants," he muttered. "That's the only reason."

Gabby smiled. "I'd love to play, but I have to get to school, too." She bent down and wrapped Trymmy in a huge hug. He stayed stiff in her arms, but Gabby wasn't bothered. She was used to that with Carmen. "I hope I get to see you sometime soon."

She released Trymmy and ran, zooming out of the Lost and Found and across the fields. She promised herself that even if she never got to sit for Trymmy again, she'd ask Edwina to arrange a way to see him. It wouldn't be hard. She was at the school often enough. She'd just clear it with Edwina first, then sneak in some extra time at the Lost and Found.

Gabby was panting hard by the time she reached Zee, who must have seen Gabby coming. She was already repacking her duffel bag.

"How'd it go?" Zee asked.

Gabby spun around to show the knapsack on her back.

"You're home!" Zee cheered. She wrapped her arms around the bag in a welcome-back hug.

The two of them were climbing onto the jet-powered surfboard when Gabby's phone rang. Gabby wouldn't have answered, but it was Alice, and Gabby was afraid she was worried. Maybe she'd forgotten about their morning conversation or missed Gabby's note.

"Hi, Mom!"

"Hi, baby. I noticed you took the cookbook."

Gabby felt a quick sting of panic, like she'd done something wrong. "Yeah, I saw it on top of the giveaway pile. Is that okay?"

Alice laughed. "Of course it's okay. How else were you going to get it to Madison? I'm just glad you checked your e-mail this morning. I was so tired when you woke me, I forgot to say anything. I thought I'd have to drive it over to you at school."

It seemed like Alice was speaking English, but the words made no sense. "My e-mail?" Gabby asked.

"Yes, so you saw Madison's. So strange, though—the one I got said she sent it at seven thirty this morning, but that can't be right or you wouldn't have seen it before you left. I'm so glad you did, though, and that you understood and grabbed the book. I do worry she might have hyped it up a little too much, you know? I mean, it *is* a collector's item, but you have to be into that kind of thing. Still, I *have* seen copies go for as much as five thousand dollars."

Nope, still sounded like gibberish.

"Um, Mom?" Gabby tried. "I don't really understand—"

"I know what you're going to say," Alice stopped her, "but I promise I won't miss it. I got it for next to nothing at a yard sale when I first started the business, and I haven't even looked at it in I-don't-know-how-many years. I wasn't even sure I'd find it in the garage. And yes, I know we could sell it ourselves and use the money for other things, but I want this MusicFest trip for you, Gabby. Your orchestra deserves it. You deserve it. For being so strong and brave and principled. It's my pleasure to help."

"Pleasure to help?" Gabby echoed. She was thoroughly confused, but she thought repeating her mom's words might somehow lead to better answers.

"With the book," Alice said. "That's why I dug it up last night, and why I e-mailed Mrs. Murray to tell her all about it and promise you'd give it to Madison at school today."

"At school today," Gabby said. She was still echoing, but clammy fingers of dread had started to crawl up her spine and over her scalp. The pieces were starting to come together, but in a way that made her completely nauseous.

"So have a great day, baby! Bye!"

"Bye," Gabby answered weakly as her mom clicked off. She held the phone away from her ear and just stared at it.

"Gabs?" Zee asked. "Gabs, is everything okay? You look green."

"I have to check my e-mail," Gabby said in a dull monotone.

"Okay," Zee said. "But if you do get sick, make sure to do it *behind* the board. It'll seriously mess up our traction if we have to ride over it."

Gabby nodded, but she wasn't really paying attention. She was reading an e-mail from Madison. It was one of her rah-rah auction blasts sent to her whole list of potential bidders from all over the world, pulled together from both the school's mailing list and from begging everyone for any and all e-mail addresses they could send her way. The subject line read: "THE MOMENT YOU'VE ALL BEEN H.O.O.T.ING FOR IS HERE!" and the body was an extended rave about Madison's long-promised secret surprise auction item—a first edition signed copy of *Joy of Cooking*, a collector's piece that would normally fetch tens of thousands

of dollars, but would go for a fraction of that at the Brensville Middle School Orchestra H.O.O.T. Auction.

That was the reason the book was out. It hadn't come from Edwina at all. It had come from Alice, who had promised it to Madison . . . who had just promised it to pretty much the entire globe.

Gabby didn't know when she'd swallowed an elephant, but she suddenly felt one deep in her throat, pressing down on her chest.

"Gabs?" Zee asked. "You okay? Now you look like you're going to pass out."

"I'll be fine," Gabby said dully. "I'll be right back."

Moving like the wind, she raced back down toward the Lost and Found.

She needed to talk to Trymmy. *Immediately.*

chapter EIGHT

"You came back! You want to play Secret Mega Orbs?"

When Gabby stormed into the Lost and Found, Trymmy had been sitting on the floor, leaning against the wall and distractedly sucking the end of a long mole. Now he was on his feet and smiling wide.

"I can't. . . ." Gabby was breathless from her sprint back to campus, and had to rest her hands on her thighs to gasp in more air. "I just need . . . to talk to you . . . I need the book back."

"What book?"

"The cookbook. I'll replace it with another one. You can

even hold my knapsack until I do." Gabby slipped the knapsack off her shoulders, took a second to dig out and pocket her keys and thumb drive, then held it out to him.

Trymmy shook his head—a move that didn't budge his tall corona of hair in the slightest. "I can't."

"Of course you can!"

"No. I *can't*. I don't even have the cookbook anymore."

"Trymmy, you have it. I just gave it to you!"

"I know," Trymmy said, pushing his glasses back up his wide-potato nose, "but it already went back to my collection."

"What?"

"Remember when your knapsack appeared after you answered the riddle?" Trymmy asked. "It's the same thing, only the opposite. When you gave me the cookbook, it poofed away into my collection."

Gabby shook her head. "That's crazy. I would have seen that. I would have noticed if I handed you a cookbook and it disappeared."

Trymmy shrugged. "Humans see what they want to see. If something doesn't make sense to them, they ignore it or pretend it's something else. How else do you think aliens have been around so long without most of you knowing we're here?"

It was a good point. Gabby couldn't guarantee that the book hadn't poofed away without her registering it. "Okay," she said, smacking her palms down on her jeans, "how do we get it back?"

Trymmy grinned mischievously. "You answer a riddle."

"Trymmy, this is important. No."

"It's not my choice," Trymmy insisted. "It's how it works. I'm a Troll. You *let* me take the book, so if you want it back, you have to answer a riddle."

Gabby scrunched her fingers into her curls with a frustrated groan, then dropped them down again. "Fine. Give me the riddle. I'll solve it right now."

Trymmy widened his magnified eyes and raised his unibrow. "Gabby! That's not how it works. You don't get the riddle right away. I'll e-mail it to you."

"When?!" Gabby wailed.

"It won't be that long," Trymmy said.

They both noticed the sudden increase in noise outside the Lost and Found. It could only mean students were pouring off the fields and filing past them toward the classrooms.

"I gotta go," Trymmy said. "You coming?"

Gabby didn't want to go anywhere without the cookbook, and she certainly didn't want to go to school and face Madison, but she didn't really have a choice. She walked out of the Lost and Found, but the minute they got outside they were met by a sweet-as-honey voice.

"Trymmy! What luck! I was going to wait for you in the classroom, but here you are!"

Gabby and Trymmy both looked up to see a smiling woman, maybe in her late sixties. She wore khaki-colored corduroy pants and a blue button-down shirt, with a long navy-blue Lion's Gate Academy cardigan over the whole ensemble. A matching wool cap was pulled low over her ears and covered all her hair. Her green eyes radiated kindness.

The woman looked oddly familiar to Gabby, but Gabby wasn't sure why.

Trymmy clearly didn't know her either. "Who are you?" he asked.

"I'm Ms. Farrell. I'm substituting for Ms. Roth today. She's ill."

Ah, that explained it. She was a substitute teacher. Subs go to all the area schools. Gabby must have seen her at Brensville.

"I have some fun stuff planned for us today," Ms. Farrell continued. "An off-campus field trip! We're working on algebra, right?"

Trymmy nodded.

"Good. So tell me"—Ms. Farrell leaned in conspiratorially—"why won't Goldilocks drink a glass of water with eight pieces of ice in it?"

Trymmy scrunched his face for a second, then his whole expression spread into a wide smile. "Because it's too cubed!"

Ms. Farrell held up her hand and Trymmy smacked it. They both laughed out loud.

Laughing at math jokes. This was clearly Gabby's cue to go. She peeked at her phone and realized her classes were starting *now.* She'd be late, but if she got back to Zee right away, they'd both still make most of first period. Or better—Gabby could slip into the computer lab and use the end of first period to print out her history paper so she'd have time to go over it before she turned it in.

"Bye, Trymmy," she said. "Talk to you *soon.*"

She pointed to him with the last word, stressing its importance, then took off at a run while he walked away in the other direction with Ms. Farrell.

Gabby had almost reached Zee when her chest grew tight. It wasn't from running. She had suddenly realized where she had seen a face like Ms. Farrell's before. The woman Gabby saw last night, the stranger who was walking her dog when Feltrymm dropped Gabby off—*she* had green eyes, too.

But that had to be a coincidence, right? Lots of people had green eyes. What really stood out about the woman with the dog was her long gray braid. Ms. Farrell didn't have a braid. She didn't even have gray hair.

Or did she? All her hair had been covered by the wool cap.

Gabby didn't even realize she had stopped in her tracks until she heard Zee calling from just up ahead.

"Gabs? What's up? Everything okay?"

Gabby didn't answer. She turned and sprinted back onto the Lion's Gate campus. She ran so fast she thought her heart would explode. All the while, she screamed at herself inside her head. Edwina had *warned* her to be vigilant. She'd *told* Gabby that people affiliated with G.E.T.O.U.T. could be watching her. She'd *specifically asked* Gabby to take pictures of anyone strange who showed up around her. But when it actually happened, Gabby didn't even notice.

Gabby tried to breathe. Maybe she was wrong. Maybe Ms. Farrell wasn't the same woman at all. Maybe she was just a fantastic substitute teacher taking a star student off campus for a more interesting tutoring session than he usually got to enjoy.

Then she saw them. Trymmy and Ms. Farrell were all the way at the front entrance of the school, walking toward the visitors' parking lot. Gabby ran even faster, ignoring the searing pain in her legs and her ragged breath. She made it to the parking lot just as Ms. Farrell was climbing into the driver's seat of a light blue compact car. Trymmy was already in the passenger's seat. Though Ms. Farrell was still about fifty yards away, Gabby could make out the back of her head as she bent down to get into her car. The wool cap had slipped upward, revealing the bottom half of a large, twisted bun of gray hair.

Gabby's heart collapsed into her stomach.

"Hey!" she screamed frantically. *"HEY!"*

But she was so breathless she barely made a sound, and so exhausted from the effort she couldn't move. Ms. Farrell's car pulled out of its spot and drove toward the school's exit. She was taking Trymmy away, and there was nothing Gabby could do.

No. There was something. Gabby pulled out her phone and clicked the camera. She zoomed in as close as possible on the car's license plate, then hit the button to take a constant blast of pictures until the car turned the corner and sped away.

Part of Gabby only wanted to collapse in a puddle and cry, but that wouldn't help Trymmy. Instead she plopped cross-legged onto the blacktop, yanked off her knapsack, and pulled out one of the tiny notebooks and pencils she kept for secret spy adventures. Trying hard to control her shaking hands, she scrawled out a message for Edwina:

Trymmy taken, I think by G.E.T.O.U.T. License plate on picture. PLEASE HELP!!!!

She took a picture of the note.

Then she sat.

She had no idea what to do next. She couldn't do anything else to reach Edwina beyond what she'd already done. She couldn't contact Trymmy's parents. She had no numbers for them, and no idea where exactly they lived.

She could only wait. So that's what she did. She sat on the blacktop and let the cold seep through the seat of her jeans and freeze her rear end.

"Gabs?"

It was Zee. Her voice sounded small and worried. It was very un-Zee-like and told Gabby she probably looked as bad as she felt.

"You okay?"

Gabby just shook her head. She kept her eyes on her lap. She didn't want to look at anyone.

"You're sitting in the middle of a parking lot," Zee said. "It's kind of not so safe."

Gabby heard the words, and part of her knew they made sense. She just couldn't fathom doing anything about them.

Zee crouched down next to her. "Want to tell me what happened?"

Gabby couldn't. What she did do was hand Zee her phone. The picture of the note she'd scrawled was still on the screen. Though Gabby didn't look, she knew Zee must have

read it because her voice had dropped an octave when she spoke again. "Oh no . . ."

There was silence between them for a moment, then Zee's face loomed right in front of Gabby's. Zee's braids hung like a curtain, blocking Gabby's peripheral vision. All she could see was Zee.

"Here's the deal," Zee said. "This is beyond big-time horrible, but you did everything you could do. And Edwina, she's like Superman, right? I mean, she showed up in your TV. She'll find this car, and she'll find Trymmy. And in the meantime, you can't stay here like this. It's not helping, and sooner or later someone from Lion's Gate is going to start asking questions you're not allowed to answer. Am I right?"

"But it's my fault," Gabby said dully. "The woman who took him, I saw her yesterday. She must have followed us here. I *led* her right to Trymmy. And now . . ."

Gabby couldn't even finish.

Zee looked pained, but rubbed a comforting hand on Gabby's back. "He'll be okay," she said. "I know it. But seriously, we've got to go."

Gabby nodded numbly. She knew Zee was right. It would only make things worse if she had to answer a bunch of questions from Gareth or anyone else at Lion's Gate. She put all her stuff back in her knapsack and hoisted it over her shoulder as she stood up . . . then nearly fell right back down.

Zee grabbed her arm. "You okay?"

Gabby nodded. "My butt fell asleep."

Zee laughed out loud. Gabby mustered up a small smile, but that was the best she could do. As the two walked back across the Lion's Gate campus to the waiting jet-powered surfboard, Gabby said, "I can't go to school. I can't concentrate until I hear. I'll e-mail in the stupid paper."

"No worries," Zee assured her. "I'll drop you at home. Your mom there?"

Gabby shook her head. "She's catering today. But I have my keys. When the school tells her I wasn't there, I'll just say I was sick."

"Cool."

"You don't have to bring me home, though," Gabby said. "You're late enough. I'll take a bus or something."

"Dude, you're so not getting out of a jet-board ride that easily. Come on."

They'd reached the board. Zee shouldered her camouflage duffel, they both put on their helmets, and they were off. When they got to Gabby's place, Zee offered to stay with her, but Gabby said no. Once inside, she trudged up to her room, e-mailed the history paper to her teacher, then slid off her chair and curled into a small ball on the closest pile of laundry.

Never in a million years would Gabby have thought she'd

fall asleep. She was too worried and heartsick and filled with self-loathing. But before she knew it she was lost in a nightmare where she was screaming at the fake Ms. Farrell, who had both Gabby and Trymmy tied to a conveyor belt, their heads moving closer and closer to the world's largest hammer.

BOOM! BOOM! BOOM!

That was the hammer. Gabby could hear it as if it were right there in the room.

BOOM! BOOM! BOOM!

Wait a minute—that wasn't the world's largest hammer at all. It was the door. Gabby's eyes eased open. "Mom?" she moaned groggily.

The door was wide open. No one was pounding on it.

BOOM! BOOM! BOOM!

That same sound again. Was it the *front* door? But it sounded so close.

"Oh for the love of Zinqual, Gabby, look over here!"

No voice could have propelled Gabby out of her laundry nest faster. She leaped to her feet and saw Edwina's angular, lined face filling Gabby's desktop computer screen. Edwina reached up a hand and tapped the screen from inside.

BOOM! BOOM! BOOM!

"Are you quite with me now?" Edwina asked.

"YES!" Gabby lunged for her desk and leaned close to Edwina's face. When Gabby spoke, her words came out in a

wild rush. "Do you have Trymmy? Is he okay? Did you get the woman? Was she G.E.T.O.U.T.? Is Trymmy okay????"

Edwina sighed, lowering her eyelids to half-mast. "What have I told you about questions? I will always tell you everything you need to—"

"But, Edwina!" Gabby wailed.

Edwina rolled her eyes. "Yes, yes, I know you're anxious. Fine, then. You'll be happy to know that Trymmy is indeed safe and sound."

Relief poured through Gabby's body and she collapsed into her desk chair. "Thank goodness."

"And thank *you*," Edwina said. "Snapping the picture of the license plate was very quick thinking. We had the woman apprehended before she was two blocks away from Lion's Gate Academy. Without you she likely would have gotten away."

"Thank you," Gabby said, leaning forward onto her desk. "Thank you for telling me and thank you for saving him. I was so scared. . . ."

"Then again, without you she likely would never have gone after Trymmy in the first place."

Gabby took a deep breath. "I know," she said, "and I am so, so, sorry—"

"Sorry isn't enough," Edwina said, her voice edged and her nostrils flaring. "I thought I had impressed upon you the importance of the Unsittables program, and of everything we do here at A.L.I.E.N."

"You did! I—"

"And I believe I expressly forbade you from contacting any of your charges outside of official babysitting jobs."

"I know," Gabby babbled desperately, "but I thought this was different. I thought you knew, and you put the cookbook out for me, and you *wanted* me to solve the riddle on my own—"

"You put a child's life in danger!" Edwina snapped.

"I know," Gabby moaned miserably. "I'm sorry. I—"

"Interesting tidbit," Edwina said, and for the first time ever Gabby noticed stray wisps of hair were flying loose from her normally tight bun. "We questioned 'Ms. Farrell,' who, *exactly* as I'd warned you, is a kook who'd seen your picture on the G.E.T.O.U.T. Web site and decided to investigate on her own. She said she first saw you last night, when you were shouting 'alien-sounding names' in the middle of a residential street."

"I can explain that," Gabby said. "It was my knapsack. My thumb drive with my history report was in it and—"

"No excuses!" Edwina leaned closer, filling the screen with her face from forehead to chin. "I know exactly why you did what you did. I even understand that you missed taking this woman's picture for us, despite the fact that I advised

you to be vigilant about strangers. What I can't understand is why you defied my orders and led this woman straight to Lion's Gate Academy, where she saw you talking to a child who is clearly human to most human beings but suspiciously different to a person seeking out aliens. While you were having your terribly important conversation with Trymmy about your precious knapsack, she cleverly asked around and got the information she needed to pass herself off as someone he could trust, and this all happened *right under your nose*."

Every word Edwina said sliced into Gabby's heart. She pulled her feet onto her chair and hugged her legs in tight. She didn't want to cry, but the tears had already built up in her throat and pooled in her eyes. She knew if she opened her mouth they'd spill out, but she couldn't just stay quiet.

"I messed up." Gabby said the words softly, hoping to keep the tears inside, but they tumbled soundlessly down her cheeks anyway. "I was so worried about my paper and the riddle . . . I believed what I wanted to believe. I figured you were the one who gave Trymmy my e-mail address and put out the cookbook, so I thought the rule about visiting didn't count. I shouldn't have done that. You gave me an order. I shouldn't have gone against it without you telling me it was okay."

"That's right," Edwina said.

"I know," Gabby said again, "and I'm so, so sorry. If

anything had happened to Trymmy because of me . . ."

She hugged her legs closer as the tears flowed faster.

Edwina sighed, leaning back from the camera. Her eyes looked tired now, and the lines in her face deeper. All of a sudden, Gabby could see every year of Edwina's advanced age.

"I understand why you jumped to the conclusions you did," Edwina admitted. "I did, in fact, give Trymmy your e-mail address, because I saw your note and knew you'd need a riddle. I observed his riddle as well, and even intended to reach out to you this afternoon to see if you'd solved it, and to facilitate you getting a cookbook to Trymmy."

This sounded so kind to Gabby that she almost couldn't bear it. "Really?" she asked.

"Really," Edwina said. Then her face stiffened. "But never did I suspect you would go against a direct command and seek the child out on your own. *Never.*"

"It'll never happen again," Gabby promised.

"I know it won't," Edwina said with a finality that made Gabby's heart stop.

"There is a very delicate relationship between A.L.I.E.N. and the Intergalactics we're sworn to protect," Edwina went on. "They need us, but we need them, too, in more ways than you can possibly know. For the balance between humans and aliens to succeed, it is vital that they trust us. They need to know that when a human is affiliated with A.L.I.E.N., that human is someone in whom they can put their complete faith. They must feel utterly confident that human has their best interests first and foremost in his or her mind, to the point where these Intergalactics feel comfortable putting their very lives—their *children's* lives—in that human's hands."

Dread curled inside Gabby's gut. She had a horrible feeling she knew what Edwina was going to say, and she didn't dare breathe for fear it would bring the news faster.

Edwina sighed. A long sigh, with her eyes closed. "I'm afraid, Gabby Duran, that you are no longer Associate 4118-25125A. As of this moment, we must terminate your engagement with A.L.I.E.N."

chapter NINE

Gabby felt the air whoosh out of the room.

Three weeks ago she hadn't even known A.L.I.E.N. existed, and now being cut off from the organization felt like being sentenced to a life without breath. She gaped like a fish in a net, her mouth trying to form words that wouldn't come out.

"Edwina," she finally managed, "please. I'll be more careful next time, I swear. Just, please, give me another chance."

A wan smile softened Edwina's face. "If it were up to me, I would, but this goes well over my head. Allynces and Feltrymm were very unhappy when they heard our report.

They demanded a rolling head. If they didn't get their way . . . Believe me when I say there are forces in play here much larger than anything you need to understand."

"So I'm out?" Gabby said, nearly choking on the words.

"We'll be lucky if it's only you," Edwina said. "At the moment, the entire Unsittables program has been suspended."

Gabby's jaw dropped and she gasped. "But all those kids! Like Philip and Wutt and Trymmy—"

"Will currently go back to being officially declared Unsittable, yes," Edwina confirmed. "Which to my thinking will cause even more big-picture problems, but that's a fight I'll be taking up with my superiors. If I succeed, it will be reinstated one day. If not . . ." Edwina's voice trailed off and her eyes looked puffy. Gabby wondered if she was trying not to cry.

It was too much. Gabby sank even lower. Her body felt like it weighed a thousand pounds.

"It's all my fault," she said.

Edwina didn't contradict her. Instead she snapped briskly back to life. "So then," she said in her regular clipped voice, "there are some details to the decommissioning process. First of all, you shall have no further contact *of any kind* with anyone already known to you as an alien, nor shall you attempt to have such contact. Should one of these aliens try to get in touch with you, you are required to terminate this attempt as swiftly as possible. To facilitate this, we have taken the liberty of blocking the e-mails and phone numbers of all your previous clients and anyone affiliated with them from your phone and e-mail accounts."

Gabby nodded numbly. She'd never known how to contact Wutt or Philip, but she'd hoped Trymmy might e-mail her so she could at least say good-bye. Now she wouldn't get the chance.

"Naturally, we also expect you to keep the secrets of A.L.I.E.N. to which you have been privy. Those who have benefitted from the indiscretions you have already made in that arena must also keep their silence."

Gabby nodded again. She knew Edwina meant Zee and Satchel. Zee would never say anything, and Satchel purposely knew so little he couldn't if he tried.

"Maintaining these requirements will stop A.L.I.E.N. from taking more drastic measures, including but not limited to Selective Memory Readjustment."

Gabby leaned forward, her hand nervously reaching up to twirl her hair. "'Selective Memory Readjustment'?" she echoed incredulously. "You mean, you'll erase my brain?"

"*Selectively* erase your brain," Edwina clarified. "Of only those moments that could put our program in jeopardy. And possibly that time in the middle of first grade when you wet your pants during the Pledge of Allegiance—if we're feeling generous."

Gabby's jaw dropped. Even now, the things Edwina said never ceased to amaze her.

Edwina smiled. "However, I have faith it won't come to that. Good-bye, Gabby Duran. It has been a pleasure."

The screen clicked off.

Gabby stared at her own reflection on the monitor . . . until it suddenly flicked back to Edwina's face.

"Oh, I almost forgot," Edwina said. "You need to get to school. You're not an associate now, and I cannot sit by and knowingly let a child cheat herself out of a day's education. Or half a day's education, such as the case may be. Your principal has your excuse for this morning, but should you continue this moping-at-home nonsense, I assure you neither he nor your mother will believe any explanation you devise."

The computer clicked off again before Gabby could respond. This time she leaned close to the screen, staring at her reflection as if it might flick again. She even tapped on the monitor, but the only result was smudgy fingerprints.

Gabby fell back into her chair.

There it was. Her career as an A.L.I.E.N. associate was over. Back to life as Gabby had always known it. She spun around in her chair, staring at her room and thinking about that life. She'd always loved it before. Why did it suddenly seem so small?

Pursing her lips together, Gabby forced herself to her feet. No matter how hollow she felt, she had to listen to Edwina's final order. She had to get to school. She changed into a fresh pair of jeans and a black-and-white flannel shirt that was soft enough to offer some comfort, then grabbed her jacket and knapsack and walked out to the garage. She had only just remembered that her bike wouldn't be there because she'd left it outside the robotics shed this morning, when she saw it sitting in its regular spot. One last helping hand from Edwina.

As she pulled out of the garage, Gabby noticed someone shuffling down the other side of the street. It was a man, maybe ten years older than Gabby's mom, wrapped in ratty wool clothes and a battered jacket. He looked oddly tan and had salt-and-pepper hair that was tamped down on one side like he'd just gotten up. He hunkered over a half-rusted shopping cart filled with recyclable bottles and cans and pushed it slowly down the block.

Something tingled at the back of Gabby's spine. Seeing the man here was odd. Gabby's development was five miles from the nearest store with a shopping cart, and Gabby had never in her life seen someone pushing one down her street. Yet that didn't bother her as much as the distinct feeling that she'd seen this man before. She stared at him until it clicked: he looked remarkably like the gardener she'd seen when she'd met Edwina yesterday—the one pruning bushes next to their meeting place, who'd seemed so disgusted by that house's shoddy landscaping. Despite the cart-pusher's apparently more difficult circumstances, he shared the same hair and build as the gardener. Could he possibly be the same person?

Gabby grabbed her phone and was about to snap a picture when she remembered she didn't have to. She wasn't affiliated with A.L.I.E.N. anymore. Any kook following her now would get nothing out of it but a glimpse into Brensville Middle School life. She pocketed her phone and wheeled away.

When Gabby got to Brensville, she locked her bike in the rack out front, then walked inside. The first person she saw nearly stopped her heart. He was an older man with white hair that grew in a low circle around his mostly bald head, who wore scruffy jeans and a tartan button-down shirt.

Mr. Ellerbee, the school janitor. He was on a ladder fixing a hallway lightbulb, though the last time Gabby had seen him he'd been riding on flying vacuum saucers and trying to destroy her.

Gabby took a deep breath and tried to calm her nerves. She reminded herself that Edwina had told her he was on A.L.I.E.N.'s side now, so she had nothing to fear. Although even if he had still been with G.E.T.O.U.T., it wouldn't impact Gabby. She was no longer A.L.I.E.N.-affiliated. She wondered how long she'd have to keep reminding herself of that.

"Hi, Mr. Ellerbee," she called out with a wave and all the fake confidence she could muster.

Ellerbee looked down but showed no specific recognition of her face. He simply smiled kindly and said, "Oh, hello," in his Scottish lilt. Then he turned back to the job at hand.

Gabby wondered if he'd already messed up with A.L.I.E.N. and had his memory Selectively Readjusted.

As she continued down the hallway, Gabby was thankful she'd arrived during lunchtime. The halls were pretty empty. She didn't feel ready to face a lot of other people. Yet just as she thought this and let herself feel the littlest bit relieved, a new layer of dread settled around her like a lead coat.

She could never have any contact with Trymmy again. That meant she could never get a new riddle, which meant she could never get back the cookbook her mom had promised Madison. It was an infinitesimal thing compared to the fate of the Unsittables program and all the alien kids who needed her, but Gabby knew Madison would make her life miserable for it.

On the plus side, Gabby was pretty sure she had reached maximum capacity for miserable, so maybe she wouldn't even notice.

She got to the cafeteria and peeked inside. Madison and

her group of fashion-doll BFFs were at a table on one side of the room, while Zee and Satchel had their own table all the way on the other side. That meant Gabby had a good shot of getting to Zee and Satch without Madison noticing. Keeping her head down, she started walking toward them.

"Hello," a Scottish accent lilted.

Gabby spun to her left and saw Ellerbee, smiling as he mopped up a spill. He wore the same scruffy jeans and tartan button-down shirt, had the same ring of white hair around his mostly bald head, and even graced her with the same kind expression, but there was no way on Earth he could be the same man she'd just passed in the hallway.

No way on *Earth*.

Hadn't Edwina said something about Ellerbee and a cloning device? If so, it was weird that no one else had noticed there were two of him walking around, but then she remembered what Trymmy had said about humans seeing only what they wanted to see. Maybe it wasn't so weird after all.

"Hi, " Gabby said back, then quickly walked the rest of the way and slipped into an empty chair at Zee and Satchel's table. Zee nearly choked on her pork roll when she saw her.

"Gabs! What happened? You hear anything?"

Gabby nodded. "He's fine."

Zee leaned her head back with relief. "Oh good. That's excellent. Totally glad to hear it."

Satchel paused with a forkful of homemade linguini from his aunt Toni's restaurant two inches from his mouth. "Me too. Whatever it was. Which I don't want to know, but I'm glad he's okay." He punctuated the sentiment by shoving the pasta into his mouth and making the loud *mmmm* sounds only merited by Aunt Toni's finest creations.

Gabby's throat turned to sandpaper as she squeezed out her next words.

"But I'm out."

"Out of what?" Satchel asked through a mouthful of noodles. "Oh, out of food! You need lunch!" With his long arms, he pushed a Tupperware container full of pasta across the table to her. "Eat. I've had a ton. It's incredible."

Zee, however, knew exactly what Gabby meant. Her mouth hung open in disbelief. "You're *out*? Like, for-now out?"

"For-good out," Gabby said, then pressed her lips together and blinked quickly to hold back blooming tears.

Satchel didn't need to know exactly what was going on to see that his friend was upset. In a single, gangly motion, he climbed over a chair to sit right next to Gabby. "Are you okay?"

Gabby blinked faster. She sniffled. Satchel was a head taller than her, but he was hunched down enough that she didn't have to look up to meet his eyes. "I will be. It was my own fault. I just . . . wish it was different."

Zee leaned in close on Gabby's other side. "But Trymmy's okay. You said that, right? And that's the most important thing."

Gabby nodded. She blinked down at the pasta Satchel had pushed in front of her. She had no desire to eat, but it was easier to keep hold of herself if she didn't keep looking directly at her friends. Out of her peripheral vision, she saw Satchel and Zee exchange glances. Zee raised her eyebrows in a silent question, and Satchel shrugged uncertainly. Then Zee cringed, as if worried about what she was about to say, but said it anyway.

"Satch and I have been comparing notes," Zee said. "That gnarly old cookbook you delivered to Trymmy . . . does it have anything to do with the signed, first-edition cookbook Madison's telling everyone is going to be the big-ticket item at the H.O.O.T. auction?"

Gabby looked from Zee to Satchel, both of them so earnest and worried for her. She nodded solemnly to answer their question . . .

. . . and then burst out laughing, so hard no sound came out.

It seemed wrong to laugh, really. The H.O.O.T. auction was a huge deal for the Brensville Middle School Orchestra, and it meant a lot to Gabby, too. But it was so much less a deal than risking Trymmy's life, or letting down Edwina, or losing the Unsittables program, that Gabby couldn't help herself. The laughter was contagious, too. After looking at each other with concern for a bit, Zee and Satchel started laughing just as hard.

"So you don't have it?" Satchel snorted as the laugh caught in his nose.

Gabby shook her head, chuckling.

"And you're out," Zee giggled, "so that means you can't get it?"

Gabby chuckled harder as she nodded her head this time.

"Madison's going to kill you," Zee snickered.

"Hard-core kill me," Gabby agreed.

"She'll kill you and *then* she'll kill you even worse!" Satchel burst.

"When are you going to tell her?" Zee asked.

"Eighth period," Satchel answered for her. "That's our next H.O.O.T. meeting."

"Yeah," Gabby said. "I guess then."

Satchel sighed and theatrically pulled out his cell phone. "Better call Aunt Toni and ask her to prep the catering for your funeral," he said. "What do you want, penne or rigatoni?"

That got them all laughing again, and by the time lunch period ended, Gabby actually felt kind of okay about everything, even if she only had two more class periods to live. As it happened, those classes breezed by. Sixth period history was a conversation about their papers, and Gabby was glad she'd had the presence of mind to e-mail hers in. Seventh period French class was spent reading scenes from a Molière play out loud. Gabby probably learned more in those two classes than she had the entire rest of the year. She was so eager to get her mind off things that she hung on the teachers' every word and asked lots of questions.

French class *was* a little tricky, since Madison shared it. She kept trying to catch Gabby's eye, but this was not the place to drop the no-cookbook bomb. Satchel covered Gabby by constantly leaning his long body between Madison and Gabby, no matter how awkward a pretzel he had to make himself to do it. When class ended, Gabby engaged Monsieur Mirabeaux in a very involved conversation about conjugations, so Madison had no choice but to leave before her. After all, Madison couldn't be late to her own H.O.O.T. meeting.

"You missed Saturday," Satchel said as he and Gabby ambled there from the French classroom, "so you haven't seen the gym all done up yet. It's pretty cool, just maybe a little owl oriented."

"Tell me about it," Gabby said. "Last night she brought me a giant owl suit."

"Oh, snap!" Satchel stopped in his tracks. His front shock of hair dropped over one eye. "You get to be Hooty? I totally wanted that job!"

"You can have it!"

"Nah, I couldn't do that to you," Satchel said, walking in his typical slight hunch as they continued toward the gym. "Besides, Madison gave me another job."

"What is it?"

"I'm on recycling," Satchel said. "I run around with a big blue bin and get people to toss their empty bottles at me."

"You mean into the bin."

"Yeah," Satchel said, "I'm sure that's what she meant."

The two of them slipped into the gym, which was abuzz with sound and motion. It looked like the whole Brensville Middle School Orchestra was already there and hard at work. Honestly, Gabby couldn't imagine what else there was to do. The place was amazing. It didn't even look like a gym. It looked like a woodland dream come true. Giant papier-mâché trees filled the corners. At irregular intervals, stuffed owls popped out of knotholes and hooted, then ducked back inside. The noises of birds, a soft breeze, and a brook babbled through the sound system. A raised rock plateau adorned with more trees made up a stage at one end of the room. Even the bleachers and spectator chairs were decorated with leaves, and blue bunting transformed the ceiling into a clear sky painted with white puffy clouds.

"I tried to tell Madison owls were nocturnal," Satchel said. "She didn't listen."

Gabby smiled, but she couldn't laugh. The place was too impressive. It wasn't just the theming either. Madison had the room ready for business. Two of the stage trees held a giant dry-erase board between them. The board was labeled HOOT LOOT! and was clearly where someone would keep a running tally of how much money was raised at the auction. A large screen sat at one side of the stage, and a long table adorned with acorns and vines held a row of computers. And since the whole event would be live streamed, Madison had a camera hooked to a computer on a small raised platform in the middle of the room, ready to record every moment that unfolded onstage.

There was a lot Gabby didn't love about Madison, but she was blown away by all the work Madison had done. Gabby felt ashamed that she'd belittled H.O.O.T.'s magnitude. It might not be life-and-death, and it might not have intergalactic repercussions, but it mattered a lot to everyone here, and that made it important. Gabby hoped like crazy that the other auction items would do better than Madison expected, and H.O.O.T. would be a wild success despite the missing cookbook.

"Okay, everyone!" Madison shouted into the microphone onstage. She held up a bright yellow piece of paper and waved it in the air. "At the end of this period I'm sending you each home with a stack of these flyers for tomorrow's auction! Wherever you go after school, whatever you do, bring the flyers and put them up *everywhere*. We'll have people all over the world participating online, but we want to get the locals, too."

Just then, Madison spotted Gabby and smiled wide. She waved her flyers wildly in the air. "Gabbers! Come on up here!"

Gabby felt sick. She did not want to do this onstage. She shook her head.

"Oh, come on!" Madison chirped. "Everyone, get her up here!"

A chorus of "Come on, Gabby!" and "Go on!" and "Go up, Gabby!" echoed through the room. The orchestra members closest to Gabby—aside from Satchel, of course—surrounded her and gently pushed her forward until she had no choice but to walk, slowly and unwillingly, up to the stage. She climbed the stairs and stood next to Madison, a strained smile on her face.

"I think I've already spilled the beans on this one," Madison began charmingly, "but *Gabby's* the one responsible for our big-ticket item, the first-edition cookbook! Now I know a cookbook doesn't sound like much, but as I said in the e-mail, this one's a major collector's item. Similar copies have sold for thousands of dollars! *Thousands!* So thank you, Gabby Duran!"

Everyone cheered. Gabby even saw Maestro Jenkins, the

orchestra's conductor, cup his hands around his mouth and cry, "Brava! Brava!"

Gabby slipped her own hands into the sleeves of her flannel and rubbed the ends of the cuffs. This wasn't going to be easy.

"So, Gabby," Madison continued, "your mom said you'd give me the book today, so let's have it!" She called to the crowd. "Don't you guys want to see it?"

Of course everyone cheered again. Except Satchel. His face was locked in a wide grimace of impending doom.

Gabby gripped her cuffs tighter, bit her lip, then leaned toward the microphone. Feedback screeched through the sound system and everyone groaned. Once that died down, Gabby tried again.

"I . . . um . . . don't have the cookbook," Gabby said.

"What?!" Madison's hiss echoed through the crowd.

"I'm really sorry," Gabby told Madison. "My mom wasn't lying. She thought we had the book . . . but we don't."

For just a second, Madison's beautiful face contorted into something hideous and zombielike. Then she smoothed herself back to perfection. By the time she spoke, she wore a smile.

"You mean, you don't *now*," Madison clarified, "but you will by tomorrow's auction."

Gabby bit her lip again, but she shook her head. "No,"

she said. "I don't have it at all. I won't. I'm sorry."

The gym rumbled with everyone's groans of disbelief. Gabby tried to slide off the stage, but Madison's shrill, pointed voice pinned her in place.

"But, Gabby, you told me *from the very beginning* that you'd have this book. That's why I stuck with the auction, because *you* told me you had a super-amazing secret item that would earn a lot of money! Without that book, we won't make enough for MusicFest . . . and it'll be *all . . . your . . . fault*!"

Gabby looked out at the crowd. Every single member of the orchestra, except Satchel, stared at her accusingly. Even Maestro Jenkins looked disgusted.

Gabby knew she could take the mic and call Madison out. She could tell everyone that Madison was lying, that Gabby had *never* promised a big secret item, that *Madison* was the one who had promised something she couldn't deliver.

But why? In a sense, Madison was right. This was Gabby's fault. If she had been a worthy A.L.I.E.N. agent and listened to Edwina about not letting Trolls steal her things, none of this would have happened. She'd have held on to her knapsack, wouldn't have needed a cookbook, and when Madison came calling for her big-ticket item, Gabby could easily have given it to her. So no, maybe Gabby wasn't guilty of Madison's *exact* accusation . . . but she was definitely guilty.

"I'm sorry," she said again. She kept her head low as she walked to the back of the gym.

"You just keep walking, Gabby Duran!" Madison barked into the mic. "And don't bother to come back for the auction. That's only for people who care about this orchestra! Satchel, you're Hooty now. You can get the costume from your so-called friend."

Madison said this just as Gabby reached Satchel, and he couldn't help but perk up like a prairie dog.

"Really?" He beamed. "I get to be Hooty?"

Gabby just looked at him.

"Right," he corrected himself. "Friend in need. Way more important."

"It's fine," Gabby said. "I'll bring you the costume in the morning."

She walked out of the gym and straight to the bike rack. This was the last period of the day. Despite Edwina's worries about missing quality education, there was no reason to stick around Brensville Middle School if she wasn't helping with H.O.O.T.

On the way home, she stopped by the playground where she'd taken Wutt, the second alien child she'd ever met. That day had marked Wutt's first time playing with humans her own age, and Gabby would never forget the girl's huge smile or the way her eyes had lit up with glee. Sure, the smile and eyes had been in rag-doll form at the time, but that didn't make their joy any less palpable. Gabby couldn't believe she'd never see Wutt again, or that she'd never be able to bring that kind of happiness to another alien child who so desperately deserved it.

Gabby was about to head home when she noticed someone on one of the playground benches. He was middle-aged, with a natural tan, perfectly groomed salt-and-pepper hair, and an air of sophistication that made it seem like he should be behind a news desk instead of in a park. He wore jeans and a light blue button-down shirt with a blazer. No one else took any notice of him, but in Gabby he triggered a memory. Her nerves prickled when she realized it. He looked like the cleaned-up twin of the man she saw earlier, the one with the shopping cart. Which meant he *also* looked uncannily like the gardener she'd seen at the house next to the one where she'd met Edwina yesterday.

Two of the men could be coincidence. Three could not. Gabby pretended to watch the kids on the seesaw, but she kept the corner of an eye on him. She was close enough to see his piercing blue eyes each time they darted toward her, which they often did. Stranger than that, he kept leaning down to mutter into his chest, like maybe he had a microphone hidden in his shirt pocket.

The Silver Fox, Gabby dubbed him in her mind: a crafty

salt-and-pepper-haired man willing to dress up in different outfits to stalk her all over town. Had she still been with A.L.I.E.N., he'd be a dangerous adversary. She was tempted to tell him he was wasting his time with her, but decided against it. He probably wouldn't believe her. Besides, Gabby thought as she pedaled home, maybe if he concentrated on her, it would keep him away from *real* A.L.I.E.N. agents and associates. So in a way, she was still doing her part to help the team.

It wasn't much, but at the moment it was all she had.

chapter TEN

When Gabby got home, she went straight to her room, lay down on her bed, and closed her eyes. She felt so drained, she thought she wouldn't wake up until morning, but the smell of incredible food lured her down for dinner, where Alice dished out a savory stew with thick, crusty bread. Carmen of course refused to let the bread touch the stew, even though dipping was half the fun. As they all dug into the meal, Alice regaled the girls with stories of her latest catering assignment: a wedding for two dogs.

"The dogs hired you?" Carmen asked.

"Their owners," Alice clarified.

"They hired you to make dog food?" Gabby asked.

"Yes!" Alice laughed. "But dog food that people can enjoy, too. Like this stew—I'm going to serve it as the main dish!"

Carmen looked at Gabby, who raised an eyebrow. That was all Carmen needed to see. She pushed the stew away.

"I'm not eating dog food," she said.

"Carmen," Alice clucked, "it's not dog food. It's perfectly good people food. I just happen to be serving it to dogs."

"Which makes it dog food," Carmen insisted.

"*Delicious* dog food," Gabby enthused, dipping in her bread for a huge bite.

It really was delicious, but torturing Carmen by savoring each bite made it even better. Gabby polished off two servings while Alice and Carmen debated the definition of dog food. Then Gabby cleared the dishes and poured some animal crackers into a big bowl, which she set in the middle of the table. Gabby and Carmen both immediately grabbed a handful.

"Animal crackers, Gabby?" Alice tsked. "Really? They're so artificial."

"They're not!" Gabby objected. "They're made from real animals!"

Carmen froze, a cracker an inch from her mouth. "That's not true," she said.

"Isn't it?" Gabby's eyes twinkled. Carmen squirmed, and Gabby knew her sister was seconds from jumping up and

racing to the animal cracker bag to be sure.

"They're not made from animals," Alice said. "And Gabby, stop teasing your sister. Tell me about the cookbook instead."

Gabby's animal crackers turned into a lump of clay in her mouth. The only good part of that was she couldn't have answered Alice even if she'd tried.

Alice didn't seem bothered. She leaned her elbows on the table and cradled her chin in her hands as she peppered Gabby with eager questions. "What did Madison say when you gave it to her? Is she excited? Is everyone excited? You know, I was thinking, I'm on some Facebook groups for chefs and if I posted something about the auction, I just know that—"

Gabby would have loved to play along and not tell Alice the truth, but it wouldn't help. Even if Alice didn't hear anything before the auction, she'd certainly find out when she showed up for the event. Gabby took a big drink of water, then blurted it out in a single word.

"MomIlostthecookbook."

That said, Gabby snatched several more cookies and shoved them into her mouth to glue it shut again.

Alice shook her head as if clearing it out. "I'm sorry," she began, "did you just say you *lost* a five-thousand-dollar book?"

"We had a five-thousand-dollar book?" Carmen repeated. "Why isn't that in my list of our assets?"

"Because we don't have it anymore, Carmen," Gabby snapped.

"Don't get snippy with your sister," Alice said. "She's not the one who lost a five-thousand-dollar book."

"I know. You're right. I'm sorry." Gabby felt like she was saying "I'm sorry" a lot these days. "I don't know how it happened. I had it in my bag this morning, and then when I looked inside to give it to Madison, it wasn't there."

This was a ridiculously awful story, Gabby knew, but she didn't have the energy to think of anything else. She hoped like crazy her mom would just go with it.

Alice raised her eyebrows. "So the book magically disappeared?"

"Impossible," Carmen said. "There's no such thing as magic."

"I don't know what happened to it," Gabby said, floundering. "Maybe my bag came unzipped. Maybe it fell out on my way to school."

"Maybe?" Alice asked. "Wouldn't you know? Was your bag unzipped when you got to school?"

"Five thousand dollars could buy us a year's worth of groceries," Carmen noted.

Gabby pressed her hands to her forehead. She tried to block out Carmen and answer her mother. "I can't remember. . . . I think so. . . . Yes? Maybe?"

"It would also cover our fall school-shopping budget for ten years," Carmen added.

Gabby leaned heavily on the table and shouted, "Stop with the factoids! We don't care! We know! It's a lot of money and I lost it!"

Some little sisters might have burst into tears if they got yelled at like that. Carmen didn't. She just stared at Gabby impassively and blinked. But that was enough to drown Gabby in guilt. She thumped her head onto the table.

"I'm sorry, Car. It's not your fault."

"I know," Carmen replied matter-of-factly. "I'm not the one who lost two years' worth of gas money."

Gabby felt Alice's hand smoothing her hair. "It's okay, baby," she said soothingly. "It's okay."

"It is?" Gabby's words were muffled by the table.

"It is," Alice assured her. Then, after a long moment she asked, "Gabby, you're not just *saying* you lost the book so we can use the money for ourselves, are—"

Gabby lifted her head before her mom was even finished. "No! It's not that at all! I know you wanted me to use the book for H.O.O.T., but it really is gone!"

Alice moved her chair closer and pulled Gabby in for a hug. "Okay," she said. "I'm sorry. I just had to ask. But you're so responsible. This kind of thing really isn't like you. Is it school? Are you stressed-out about work?"

This seemed like Gabby's only reasonable out, so she took it. She made up a story about school getting harder, and midsemester progress reports coming out, and the huge pressure of the just-turned-in history paper. Alice said she understood and promised to help Gabby with whatever she needed so she wouldn't get overwhelmed. As for the book, Alice told Gabby not to worry about it. Accidents happened, and if it *did* fall out of Gabby's bag, there was still a chance someone would find it, know it was the book from Madison's mass e-mail, and get it back to the H.O.O.T. auction.

Gabby, of course, knew this was impossible, but since she couldn't explain why, she simply let it go. She went to bed early that night. The last thing she thought before she fell asleep was that if there was one okay thing to come out of her being decommissioned from A.L.I.E.N., it was that she could stop lying to her mom and Carmen.

The next day was H.O.O.T., and Gabby knew she should tell her mom and Carmen that she wouldn't be the one in the Hooty outfit, but she couldn't do it. She'd had enough scrambling for explanations for a while, and besides, it was impossible to tell *who* was in the Hooty suit once it was on. If they didn't pay close attention to the bird's height, they could totally believe it was Gabby wearing it and not Satchel. She'd just have to ask him to maybe do her a favor and not unmask at the end.

Gabby dreaded seeing Madison on the bus that morning, but it turned out luck was with her. Madison wasn't there. Her mother must have given her a ride for the big day.

Yet once Gabby got to Brensville Middle School, her luck ran out. At least three orchestra members "accidentally" tripped her as she walked down the hall, two attached LOSER signs to her back, and one affixed a note to her locker that said FRENCH HORNS BLOW. Given that that's exactly what French horns do when used properly, Gabby tried to tell herself the note was simply a statement, not an insult.

Once Gabby delivered the Hooty suit to Satchel, she, Satch, and Zee slipped outside. The fall morning was cold enough that most students were staying indoors until class started, so this seemed like a good place for Gabby to avoid further harassment.

"How long do you think they'll hate me?" Gabby asked.

Satchel thought about it. "How many more years until college?"

Just then, something small and round bounced off the top of Satchel's head. He winced and his hand flew to the spot.

"Oh snap!" he complained to Zee. "It was a joke. You didn't have to hit me."

"How could I have hit you?" Zee held up her hands, which were completely occupied with chunks of her robot-in-progress.

"You threw something at me with that remote control thingy," Satchel said.

"It's a vise-clamp hand, not a remote control," Zee shot back. "And even if it was a remote, it wouldn't be a 'thingy.'"

Gabby wasn't listening to either one of them. She'd followed the small, round projectile with her eyes as it bounced off Satchel's head. It had landed among some leaves in front of him. Gabby bent down and gently ran her fingers through the fall foliage until she felt something cold and hard. She picked it up. It was a red marble with a yellow flare in the middle.

Gabby's blood rushed faster. She wasn't sure if she did or did not want to see what would be waiting for her when she looked up.

She tilted her neck back. Clinging to the outside wall of the school, only six feet or so above Satchel's head, was Trymmy, his thick claws sunk deep into the brick. His head was pointed downward, and gravity made his larger moles droop pendulously from his face. When Gabby met his eyes, he grinned and waggled his head back and forth, purposely making the moles shimmy and dance.

Gabby spoke to Zee and Satchel, but she didn't take her eyes off Trymmy. "Satch, unless you want to see something you will never be able to un-see, I suggest you head inside."

This may have been the wrong thing to say. Immediately,

both Zee and Satchel snapped their heads back to follow Gabby's gaze.

"Dude!" Zee enthused. She dropped her work to the ground and whipped out her phone, clicking the camera open. Gabby reached out and grabbed it out of her hands.

"Zee, you can't!"

"But Gabs, *look*!"

Now that he had an audience, Trymmy was showing off. He turned in wild circles along the wall, then released his fingers and let his toe claws hold him as he extended his body out like a flagpole.

"Stop!" Gabby hissed up to him. "Someone could see you!" Then, realizing three people had clearly *already* seen him, she added, "Someone *else*."

"I think my brain just melted."

It was Satchel. He was frozen in place, his neck craned back, his eyes wide. If Gabby looked closely enough, she could see the fibers of his sanity unraveling.

"Zee," Gabby said, "you've got to go. You have to take care of Satchel."

"You can't be serious," Zee said. "Do you not see what's going on up there?"

"I *am* serious!" Gabby insisted. "None of us want our memories erased."

"I do," Satchel said numbly.

Gabby raised her eyebrows at Zee, urging her to leave. Zee rolled her eyes.

"Fine. But you seriously owe me." She moved to Satchel and placed one hand on his back and one on his arm, easing him toward the door. "Come on, Satch. Easy does it. You can fall asleep in class and pretend this was all a dream."

Once they disappeared inside, Trymmy leaped off the building, did a triple somersault in midair, and landed at Gabby's feet. "Ta-da!"

"SHHHHHH!" Gabby hissed. She looked around frantically. A.L.I.E.N. and G.E.T.O.U.T. could be anywhere. She leaned close to Trymmy and whispered, "You can't be here. I can't be seen with you."

Behind his glasses, Trymmy's eyes widened with hurt and surprise. Then he just looked defeated.

"Right," he said. "You're a human. Of course you don't want to be seen with me."

"No, that's not what I mean! Not at all! But, Trymmy, people have been watching me. People like Ms. Farrell. And A.L.I.E.N. fired me. If they see me with you, I'll get in huge trouble. You have to go!" Gabby stopped herself, then asked, "Wait . . . how did you even get here?"

"I'm homeschooled now," Trymmy said, "but my new teacher's super-old and fell asleep, so I snuck out and rode my bike."

He grinned, proud of himself, but all Gabby could think was how dangerous it had been for him to be all alone in a world crawling with potential Ms. Farrells. She couldn't send him back on his own, but she couldn't escort him home either, and she *certainly* couldn't let him stay anywhere near her.

She needed to find someplace safe where she could think.

When the idea came to her, she wasn't sure if it was brilliant or completely insane. But there was a man close by who knew all about aliens, and who was working closely enough with A.L.I.E.N. that he wouldn't hurt Trymmy, but ideally not so close that he'd automatically report Gabby and Trymmy for being together.

The fact that this man had tried to kill her the last time they hung out put only a slight damper on Gabby's conviction.

"Come with me," Gabby whispered. "And stay close."

With Trymmy at her side, Gabby opened the door to Brensville Middle School and peered in. The halls were empty. First period had already started. Gabby could only hope things stayed that way as she and Trymmy made the long walk to her destination at the other end of the building.

They made it halfway across. That's where the main entrance of Brensville sat, in the very center of the school's long hall. The large glass wall and doors were on Gabby's left as she walked, so she kept Trymmy on her right. She

also peered out toward the doors before she crossed that vast central area, and made sure no cars were pulling up to drop off latecomers. Gabby truly thought she was safe as she hustled Trymmy along to the other side of the main hall, until she heard the worst sound ever.

"Gabby Duran, what are you doing out of class?" Madison Murray squealed.

Gabby made her body as wide as possible as she wheeled toward Madison. She even held out her arms to try to hide every bit of the Troll behind her.

"Madison!" Gabby squeaked. "What are *you* doing out of class?"

"*I* have a late pass," Madison crowed. "I got permission from Maestro Jenkins to put up more flyers for H.O.O.T. around town this morning. When the auction crashes and burns, at least I'll be able to say I did everything I could."

Gabby felt sweat tickle her upper lip. She hoped Madison would think it was her own intimidating presence that made Gabby nervous and wouldn't realize Gabby was keeping something from her.

"Good plan," Gabby said. "Totally. See you this afternoon in French class!"

She gave Madison a huge smile and waited for the girl to leave, but Madison didn't move. Instead she scrunched her perfectly arched eyebrows and clip-clopped her low-heeled shoes closer to Gabby. Gabby leaned back, hoping to keep Trymmy hidden.

"You're acting weird," Madison proclaimed. "Even for you. What are you hiding?" Madison's eyes grew round with realization. "It's the cookbook, isn't it? You have it!"

Madison lunged to the left, but when Gabby lunged that way to block her, Madison made a quick change and ran around Gabby on the right.

On top of everything else, Madison had catlike reflexes. Gabby promised herself she'd remember that in the future.

Gabby wheeled around, already floundering for ways she'd explain Trymmy . . . but Trymmy wasn't there. Aside from Gabby and Madison, the hall was empty.

Where had Trymmy gone? Could someone have snatched him away from right behind her? Gabby wanted to run down the halls screaming his name, but that would only make matters worse.

"See?" Gabby said with forced cheer. "Nothing there."

Madison's face pinched in suspicion. She folded her arms tightly over her ruffled blue blouse.

"You're keeping secrets, Gabby Duran," she said. "I told you before I'd find out what you're up to, and I will."

As her nemesis spoke, Gabby noticed something high up in her peripheral vision: a child-size figure crawling out from behind a trophy case.

So that's where Trymmy went. He must have jumped behind the case when he heard Madison, then crawled up the wall. Now he was scuttling down from ceiling height but stopped just a couple feet above Madison's head.

"Are you even paying attention to me, Gabby Duran?" she demanded.

"Of course! I totally am!" Gabby insisted. But she was really paying attention to Trymmy, who clung to the wall with his toe claws, folded his arms against his chest, and tossed his head in a perfect Madison imitation. Gabby had to bite hard on her cheeks so she wouldn't laugh.

Madison huffed and moved her hands to her hips, with no clue that her every move was being mirrored on the wall behind her.

"You're lucky this isn't my hall monitor period and I have to get to class," she huffed. "Otherwise I'd take you to Principal Tate myself and you could explain to *him* what you're doing."

Above her, Trymmy shook his finger scoldingly and arranged his already unusual features into a mask of cartoonish disapproval as he mouthed Madison's words along with her.

"But you *do* have to get to class, right?" Gabby reminded her. "You said you have a late pass, not a free period pass. Wouldn't want to see you get in trouble."

Madison's pink lips crunched into a puckered line. "No," she agreed. "We wouldn't. I'll leave the getting in trouble to you." She wheeled on a heel and flounced down the hall, turning back to add, "How is the orchestra treating you? Not so great, right? If you ask me, your only smart move is to drop out. That or bring me the cookbook. Toodles."

She waggled her fingers, then strode away.

"Good thing I came to your school," Trymmy said, hitting the floor and wiping wall dust off his khaki pants. "Sounds like you need that cookbook."

What Gabby needed was to get Trymmy someplace less conspicuous before first period ended and the halls filled with people. She grabbed Trymmy's hand.

"Run with me," she whispered. "*Now.*"

They sprinted down the hall in the opposite direction of Madison and didn't stop until they were right outside Mr. Ellerbee's janitorial closet. Unfortunately, Ellerbee's space was directly across the hall from Principal Tate's office, and Gabby and Trymmy hadn't exactly been light on their pounding feet.

"Who's running in the halls during class?" Principal Tate's voice wailed from behind his door, and Gabby heard the screech of his chair pushing back from its desk. Frantically, she yanked open Ellerbee's door, shoved Trymmy inside, then followed him. She shut and locked the door just as Principal Tate's door opened behind them.

The closet was tiny, and Trymmy and Gabby found

themselves practically in the lap of a small man with a white fringe of hair around his otherwise bald head. The man sat tilted back in the room's one chair, hands clasped behind his neck. His feet were propped up on the lower shelf of a unit crowded with cleaning supplies and his few personal items. He wore the exact same outfit as yesterday: jeans and a tartan shirt.

"Why hello, wee ones!" he lilted in his Scottish brogue.

"Hi!" Trymmy said.

Someone banged on the door. The knob rattled.

"Ellerbee!" Principal Tate boomed. "I heard a student running down the halls. Is someone in there?"

Gabby spoke quickly to the man who looked like Ellerbee. "You're a clone, aren't you?" Gabby asked him. "I need the real Ellerbee. Is he around?"

"Ellerbee?" the principal's voice called again from outside the door.

"One moment!" Clone-Ellerbee called. Then he winked at Gabby and Trymmy, got up from his chair, and reached for a plastic bucket on a high shelf. When he tipped the bucket forward, a square of linoleum flooring slid open to reveal a carpeted stairway. Clone-Ellerbee smiled and nodded down to it.

Principal Tate banged on the door again.

"Go on with you," Clone-Ellerbee urged quietly. "Right quick now."

Once Gabby and Trymmy had descended several steps,

the panel slammed shut above them. Gabby's ears immediately felt thick and full of cotton.

"Soundproof room," a Scottish brogue called up from below. "Plays with yer ears at first. Yeh'll get used to it. Come on down. I won't hurt you. Not getting paid to these days."

Trymmy looked questioningly at Gabby. She nodded confidently, even though she wasn't at all positive she'd made a good choice. The two of them descended the stairs and saw the exact same nearly bald man they'd seen up above, only this one wore a full kilt and a well-worn black T-shirt with a picture of the Loch Ness Monster and the words I BELIEVE on it. Like the clone above, he leaned back in his chair with his feet up, but the chair down here was thick leather, and his feet weren't on a dinky shelving unit but a massive computer console. The console jutted out below a collection of giant screens flashing so many different programs that Gabby got dizzy trying to make sense of them all. The room's other furnishings included a refrigerator, stove, microwave, hot tub, and several structures that looked like giant black marble works of abstract art, all folds and curls. She wondered if one of them was the cloning machine.

"Welcome to my humble abode," Ellerbee said. "Put it in over the weekend, your people did."

"A.L.I.E.N. did this?" Gabby asked.

"Aye," Ellerbee said. "Carved the whole room out of

nothin'. Little present for me, along with the clones to do my cleanin' work. All I do in return is stick close with those G.E.T.O.U.T. types, poke around their Web site, give your people a heads-up if anything goes awry." He kicked back from the computer console, rolling his leather chair across the room to the fridge. "Want some haggis? I can warm one in the microwave. Nothing like a little sheep entrails in a stomach casing to get the blood flowing, eh? You and yer Troll friend might like a bite."

"How do you know I'm a Troll?" Trymmy asked.

"Yeh're in the database," Ellerbee said, rolling back to the console so he could tap a few computer keys. "Not you specifically, but yer kind."

One of the big screens on the wall flickered to show a drawing of a short, hunched-over humanoid with a thick brow, pickle-shaped nose, and skin mottled with moles so large they looked like small planets. Trymmy stepped closer to the screen to stare at it. Gabby couldn't blame him. It was a pretty insulting representation.

Yet when Trymmy spoke, his voice was full of awe. "Grandma?"

Once again, Gabby reminded herself never to make assumptions about alien life. She turned her attention to more pressing matters.

"Mr. Ellerbee," Gabby said, "can I ask you to please not

say anything to A.L.I.E.N. about the two of us being here?"

"If it's not on the list of things they pay me to do, I don't do it, I can promise you that. All I ever wanted was a life of leisure, and now that's just what I've got. I even have time to take up the bagpipes! Wanna hear?"

Before Gabby could answer, he reached under the desk, pulled out the massive instrument, and began to play, filling the room with off-key bovine wails. The sound was a crime against music, but it would give Gabby and Trymmy some privacy. She leaned down to look him in the eye.

"Okay, we need to get you home like *now*, but I can't be seen with you, and I don't like the idea of you going alone. Do you have your cell phone? Can you call your parents to pick you up? They don't have to know you were with me."

"You're just going to get rid of me?" Trymmy asked. "Aren't you even going to ask why I came and found you?"

Gabby sighed. She didn't mean to be impatient, but she couldn't help thinking that Edwina could show up at any minute, memory eraser in hand. For a moment Gabby wondered if the erasing would hurt, but then she realized even if it did, the pain was probably one of the things she'd forget.

"You're right," she admitted, "I should have asked. Why did you come find me?"

"To give you this."

He pulled a piece of folded paper from his pocket and

gave it to Gabby. She opened it. The words were laid out like a poem, but Gabby knew what it had to be.

"A riddle," she said.

Trymmy nodded. "I tried e-mailing it, but the e-mails bounced back. I tried calling you, too, but you never answered."

"I would have, I promise," Gabby assured him, "but I never got the calls. A.L.I.E.N. must be blocking you. It's my own fault. I messed up. Big-time. You could have gotten really hurt because of me, and now A.L.I.E.N. won't let me see or talk to you ever again."

Gabby winced as she said that last part. It felt like she was smacking Trymmy with her words, and Trymmy reacted like she'd done just that. He recoiled and scrunched up his face in disgust.

"How is that fair?" he asked. "You're not the one who took me away from school. And it's not even like anything bad happened. They got Ms. Farrell right away!"

"But what if they hadn't?"

"But they did!" Trymmy pooked out his lower lip in a pout that covered the tip of his nose. "Do you even know why I took your backpack in the first place?"

"Of course I do," Gabby said. "Trolls steal."

"Yeah, but it's not like we *have* to steal. I took it . . ." He lowered his head and told the last part to the floor. "I took it so I could see you again. I like playing with you. I thought we

were friends." A big sigh, then he added more softly, "And I don't have any other friends."

Gabby could actually feel her heart melting down into her body. More than anything, she wanted to hug him. She wanted to tell him he was right, they *were* friends, and she'd come over and play with him whenever he wanted.

But she couldn't.

"I'm sorry," Gabby said. "I wish things were different, but they're not."

Trymmy lit up with an idea. "But we can *make* it different! We can be secret friends and play together anyway! We'll meet right here. I can come over through that Holobooth!"

He pointed to one of the more tubular black marble fixtures in Ellerbee's man cave.

"That's a Holobooth?"

"Ours is underground so you couldn't see its shape, but, yeah, that's what they look like," Trymmy said. "And you can use them to travel. Just step into a Holobooth, think real hard about another Holobooth, and you can go there. So I can come here and meet you whenever we want!"

Trymmy was so excited he bounced up and down, and his grin was infectious. Part of Gabby was dying to say yes and start planning their adventures, but she knew there was no way.

"I can't," she said. "Even if A.L.I.E.N. said it was okay,

which they *won't*, your parents don't want you around me. I can't go behind their backs. It's not right."

Trymmy opened his mouth to object, but no words came out. He just stared up at Gabby, his eyes suddenly so sad and hopeless that Gabby had to look away. She refolded his riddle and handed it to him. "You should probably take this back," she said. "I shouldn't really hold on to anything from you."

Trymmy held the paper a moment, then darted to Ellerbee's console and grabbed a pen. He scrawled something beneath the riddle. "This is my cell," he said, "and it's a number A.L.I.E.N. doesn't have. I know they're here to protect us and all, but my parents still like us to keep some things to ourselves. If you call from a phone that's not yours, A.L.I.E.N. won't know."

He held out the paper, but Gabby shook her head. "Trymmy, I can't."

"Just take it. Maybe you'll change your mind." He shrugged sadly, then added, "And if not, you'll have something to remember me by."

That was too much. Gabby threw her arms around Trymmy and hugged him tight. He stiffened, but Gabby wouldn't have expected anything else. When she pulled back she took the paper from him.

"Only because you really want me to," she explained. "Not because I need it to remember you."

Trymmy nodded. "So now what?"

"You said you can travel through the Holobooth, right?" Gabby asked. "Does that mean you can take it home?"

"Yeah," Trymmy sighed.

With his back slumped, he trudged to the Holobooth. The thing looked completely solid to Gabby, but he pressed some invisible trigger spots until a small portal slid open, then stepped inside. Magnified by his glasses, his eyes were two giant pools of melancholy. They caught Gabby's and wouldn't look away until the Holobooth door slid closed and cut them off.

As the booth hummed to life, Gabby folded Trymmy's riddle and put it in her jeans pocket. She felt something else in there and pulled it out. It was the red marble with the yellow flare, the one Trymmy had thrown down from the school wall to get her attention.

Gabby ran to the Holobooth and banged on it. "Trymmy! Trymmy, wait! You forgot someth—"

The booth stopped humming. Its panel slid open to reveal only emptiness inside.

Trymmy was gone, and Gabby would never see him again.

chapter ELEVEN

"You were his only friend and now he can't see you anymore?" Zee marveled as she fussed with some wiring on what looked like a tiny military tank. "That's awful."

Gabby had left Ellerbee's den in time for her second period class. Now it was morning break, and she, Zee, and Satchel were spending the twenty minutes hunkered in a corner of the hall. This had two benefits. First, Gabby was tucked away enough that she was less likely to face further retribution from vengeful orchestra members. Second, it kept Satchel away from the outside of the school, which he

was afraid was now crawling with thick-clawed spider-children.

"Yeah, that's seriously raw," Satchel agreed.

Gabby had her feet on the floor and her knees hugged tight, but now she peered up at Satchel in amazement. "Satch, are you actually listening to this conversation?"

"Half-listening," Satchel pointed out. "Only to the parts that sound kind of not totally insane."

"Fair enough."

"So what are you going to do?" Zee asked.

"What *can* I do?" Gabby asked back. "I mean, even if he was a regular kid, if his parents don't want me around, I can't be around. And even if they *did* want me around, it's not great for someone's babysitter to be their only friend, right?"

"Probably not ideal," Zee said. She put the tank on the floor, then pulled a remote out of her pocket and made the tank roll toward Gabby. "Unless it was a robot babysitter. Then it'd be pretty cool."

"What would you do about the kid if he weren't, you know . . ." Satchel spun his entire lanky body in an exaggerated spy-scan of the teeming halls, then leaned in and lowered his voice to just above a whisper. ". . . *what he is.*"

"Good you whispered that," Zee chided him. "Super-incriminating words."

Gabby tilted her head back and considered his question. "If he was just another kid, I'd try to help him meet other

friends. I'd take him to the playground, or the park, or we'd just ride bikes around where I knew we'd see other kids. Then I'd introduce him around until he found someone he clicked with. And he *would*—kids always do—I've seen it happen a jillion times. The perfect friend for Trymmy would just have to be really specific. Someone who isn't huggy or hand-holdy, who loves games with a lot of rules, who's hyper-crazy smart and doesn't get their feelings hurt easily, who's so super-logical they can figure out riddles in their sleep . . ."

Gabby suddenly realized both Zee and Satchel were looking at her with wide eyes and dropped jaws.

"Oh snap," Satchel breathed.

"What?" Gabby asked.

"Gabs, listen to yourself," Zee said. "Don't you realize who you're describing?"

Gabby ran over the list in her mind, and soon her own eyes and jaw mirrored her friends'.

"Holy macaroni," she intoned.

She sat up tall on crossed legs and jangled her knees up and down. Now that she'd realized it, she wanted it to happen *now*. It was perfect!

"But how? How do I get them together? Even if I somehow arrange for them to get to the same place at the same time, I know them. They'll never talk to each other on their own. I'd have to be there, and he can't be seen with me."

"I've got it!" Satchel snapped. "An invisibility potion!"

Zee rolled her eyes. "There's no such thing as an invisibility potion."

"Oh yeah?" Satchel countered. "How about kids with claws who climb walls and people who talk to you out of the TV? Is there such a thing as those?"

"That was one you probably should have whispered," Zee pointed out.

Satchel blushed and hunched over, abashed. "Sorry. Just sayin'."

"No, you're right." Gabby's eyes danced as the idea came together in her head. "I need something that'll make me invisible . . . *like the Hooty suit*!"

"That would totally work!" Satchel cried. Then he frowned. "Except I get to be Hooty." Zee elbowed him in the ribs. "I mean, unless you need the suit more," he added. "Then you can totally be Hooty. No problem at all."

He sighed heavily, but Gabby didn't have time to feel bad about dashing his owl dreams. More pieces were clicking together in her head.

"This is good," Zee encouraged her. "Now how will you get Trymmy to H.O.O.T.?"

"He gave me that number," Gabby said. "He wants to see me. I could probably just ask him."

Gabby suddenly reeled back and gasped like she'd been shot.

"Gabs?" Zee worried.

"You okay?" Satchel asked.

"So, so, *so* okay!" Gabby nearly shouted. Then she lowered her voice back to an excited hiss. "You guys, I can tell him to come to H.O.O.T. for the answer to the *riddle*! And if we give him the answer there, he'll give us the cookbook!"

Zee grinned. "Which you can give to Madison during the auction!"

"And save our MusicFest trip!" Satchel finished.

The bell rang for class. They knew they had to get up and leave, but they were too wired to move.

"Let's see the riddle, quick," Zee said.

Gabby pushed her rear off the floor so she could dig into her jeans pocket and pull out the paper. Satchel and Zee huddled on either side of her so they could all read it together.

I never was, am always to be,
No one ever saw me, nor ever will see.
I can't be bought, I can't be sold,
The young have more of me than the old.
And yet I am the hope of all
Who live and breathe on your terrestrial ball.

Bring me this riddle's answer, I pray,
And get what you seek without any delay.

"Anything?" Gabby asked hopefully.

"Not yet," Zee said. "Let's think about it during math."

"I'll think about it, too," Satchel said. "It'll be easy. I have a free period."

"That's great!" Gabby exploded with another idea. "Spend it in the library, and look up anything you can find about Trolls and riddles."

Zee tilted her head dubiously. "You think he'll find the answer there?"

"No, but Edwina told me the stuff we know as folk tales is based on real interactions with aliens," Gabby said. "Maybe Trolls have a pattern, a certain kind of riddle they always like to ask. Or maybe they look for answers that are kind of similar."

"Maybe," Zee agreed. "Worth a try."

By now the halls were empty, and they had to run to class to avoid a late slip. Yet before they did, Gabby borrowed Zee's phone and used it to text a quick note to the number Trymmy wrote on the paper.

I have the answer to your riddle, it said. *Please find a way to come to the H.O.O.T. auction at Brensville Middle School, 4 P.M–6 P.M. Try not to come alone—I want you to stay safe!*

Knowing Trymmy, Gabby was sure he'd text back before

she could even hand the phone back to Zee . . . but he didn't.

"How do we even know if he saw it?" Zee asked.

"I guess we don't," Gabby said. "We just have to hope."

She also had to hope that if he *did* see it, he'd show up. In the meantime, Gabby needed to crack the riddle. She spent math class sitting in the very back row with Zee, where they tuned out Ms. Emery and worked. For thirty-nine minutes of a forty minute class, they successfully passed notes back and forth, mulling over the possibilities of each riddle line, and their teacher had no idea.

Or so they thought.

"What is the ratio," Ms. Emery said several decibels louder than anything she'd said throughout class, "of time in minutes that Gabby Duran and Stephanie Ziebeck spent chatting with each other today to their time spent participating in class?"

When Ms. Emery finished the question, she was standing right between Gabby's and Zee's desks. Both girls sat up straighter and faced forward like the model students they were *not*, and a hot blush coated their cheeks.

"Yes, Margo?" Ms. Emery called to one of the many students with their hands high in the air.

Margo del Vecchio, one of Madison Murray's little minions, chirped, "The ratio of time in minutes that Gabby Duran and Stephanie Ziebeck spent chatting with each other today

to their time spent participating in class is thirty-seven to two."

"Good answer, Margo," Ms. Emery said, "but would you really give them the two? It seemed to me they were paying attention for only point-five minutes. Anyone else have thoughts?"

"I saw Zee stare at the active board for a minute," one girl said, "but I'm not sure if she was paying attention or thinking about something else."

"I could hear them whispering the whole time," added a boy in the front row, "so I'd say they were paying attention for zero minutes."

"I counted twenty notes passed between them," another boy said, "and if each note takes one-point-five minutes to read and respond to, that's thirty minutes."

With each comment, Gabby and Zee sank lower in their seats. When the class bell rang, Ms. Emery put one hand on each of their desks and leaned in close.

"When you waste school time, you don't learn, you don't do well on tests, you don't get good grades, you don't get into college, you don't get a good job, and you don't succeed in life. If you don't mind that, by all means, have more days like today. It's only your future."

Yikes.

Gabby said good-bye to Zee and went to the library for her next period, which she had free. She curled into one of

the big reading armchairs, but she had trouble thinking. She was too mortified by Ms. Emery's words, which now echoed in her head.

It's only your future.

It's only your future.

Future.

"Future!"

Gabby shot upright and cried the word out loud, then realized every head in the room had swiveled to face her. She smiled sheepishly.

"Future . . . tense," she explained lamely. "Studying French."

No one seemed to care. They turned away with annoyed clucks and sighs. Once their attention was off her, she yanked Trymmy's riddle out of her pocket and climbed back into the chair, legs tucked under her and feet on the seat like she was preparing to spring off. When the period ended, she couldn't get to the cafeteria fast enough.

"'I never was, am always to be,'" she recited once she, Zee, and Satchel were gathered over trays of tacos so good that Satchel was totally ignoring his home-packed meal. "That's the future. 'No one ever saw me, nor ever will see.' You can't see the future. 'I can't be bought, I can't be sold.' You can't buy or sell the future. 'The young have more of me than the old.' The young have more of a future, because they're

younger. 'And yet I am the hope of all who live and breathe on your terrestrial ball.' Everyone hopes for things in the future! That's the answer! The answer is 'the future'!"

"Oh snap!" Satchel said around a mouth full of ground beef. "That totally works!"

Instead of her food, Zee chewed on the end of one of her braids. "It's awesome, Gabs, but isn't there a last part?"

"'Bring me this riddle's answer, I pray, and get what you seek without any delay'?" Gabby asked.

"Yeah, that. How do you bring someone the future?"

Gabby twirled a curl around one of her fingers. "Not sure," she finally admitted. "Satch, did you find anything when you were looking stuff up?"

Satchel snorted. "Only that you should never mess with Trolls. Most of the stories go like this: A Troll offers this crazy amazing prize to a person if the person can answer a riddle. If the person gets it wrong, they have to pay up something huge, like all their money, or their kingdom, or their firstborn kid. But the prize is so super-awesome and the Trolls seem so warty and hunchbacky and un-smart, the person always says, 'Yeah, I'm in, riddle me up.' And every time, the riddle's this mega-impossible harder-than-*Moby-Dick*, no-way-to-get-it tangle that the person gets wrong, and the Troll takes everything."

"Which is kind of what we already knew," Gabby said.

"Yeah," Satchel agreed. "The only chance a person ever has with a Troll is to turn everything around and give *the Troll* a riddle so hard it stumps him. If that happens, then *boom*, the Troll has to give back everything he's ever taken from anyone ever. Pretty cool, right? From the stories I saw, it's happened, like, twice, in forever."

"It's interesting, sure," Zee said, "but it doesn't tell us anything about getting the future so we can give it to Trymmy."

Gabby sighed, knowing Zee was right. "I guess the bright side is that everyone already knows I messed up and the cookbook's gone. It's not like they'll be shocked if we can't figure this out and I don't get it back for the auction."

That's when Satchel started whistling and looking up at the corners of the room. Even if Gabby hadn't known him since birth, she'd have known he was hiding something. *What* he was hiding became evident maybe five minutes later, when two orchestra members, trombonist twins Eddy and Teddy Yadrinsky, stopped by the table on their way to get dessert. They wore huge matching smiles as they leaned in on either side of Gabby.

"I knew all along you were just messing with us, Gabby," Teddy said.

"Yeah," Eddy agreed. "No way would you do anything to screw up MusicFest."

They patted her on the back in unison, then walked away

without waiting for a reply, their smiles even sunnier for having spoken to her.

Satchel had now gone from whistling to *humming* at the corners of the room. With his pointed nose, he looked like a giant, off-key songbird.

"Satch?" Gabby asked.

She was distracted by a pair of arms wrapping around her shoulders, pulling her head into someone's chest.

"Gabb-eeeeeee!"

The someone broke off the hug and knelt down next to Gabby's chair. It was Lilah Hartmann, a clarinet player who had the school's longest hair. She'd never cut it in her life and it hung down her back in a long, dark braid.

"I'm so, so, so, so, so excited you're bringing the cookbook to H.O.O.T.! I already texted my mom, and she's in this online cooking group that's going *crazy* for it! I just know we'll get enough money for MusicFest now!"

She gave Gabby another giant hug, then skipped back down the aisle.

This time when Gabby turned to Satchel, he was staring at something deeply fascinating he'd discovered under one of his fingernails.

"Forgive me, Gabby," a voice rang out, "I never should have doubted you."

That voice Gabby knew well. She winced inside, but

pasted on a huge smile to face Maestro Jenkins, the head of the Brensville Middle School Orchestra.

"Hi, Maestro."

"I was so distraught when I first heard that you'd pulled the book out of the auction. I have to admit, I was starting to wonder about your commitment to our orchestra. That was wrong of me. I look forward to planning our MusicFest trip, and to your considerable part in the concert we play there." Maestro Jenkins took Gabby's hands in his, held them just a moment—were there tears in his eyes?—then strode back to his own table.

Gabby scanned the room to make sure no one else was coming for her. No one was, but way too many orchestra members were looking her way with giddy smiles on their faces.

She slipped out of her seat and under her table before any more of them could approach. The cafeteria floor was grimy with dust and random stickiness, and the underside of her table was blobbed with unnamable ancient dried foodstuffs. Gabby stayed low so her curls wouldn't catch in any of it. She crawled across to Satchel's long, denim-clad legs, and tugged on them until he joined her. Being so much taller, he had to scrunch into a small ball and his top flap of hair totally grazed something that once was a pork roll, but Gabby wasn't concerned.

"What did you do?" she hissed.

"I couldn't help it," he said. "When I was walking to my last class, Andrew Lewis was talking dirt about you to, like, half the brass section, and I got mad. I pulled him aside and told him you *did* have the book, and he should expect it to appear by the end of the auction."

"Why would you say that?"

"I told you! I didn't like the way he was talking about you."

"But now everyone's expecting me to have the book!" Gabby wailed.

"Well, you will. You figured out the riddle."

"Not how to give it to him! And what if I'm wrong? Or what if Trymmy doesn't even show up?"

"Then you're in huge trouble," Zee admitted, slipping under the table to join the conference. "The stuff you dealt with this morning will be nothing. They'll be out for blood. Speaking of which . . ." She looked suspiciously up at a red blotch just over her head on the underside of the table. "We've really got to get out of here."

Sliding under the table was a lot easier than sliding back out. Gabby had to contort her body to get around the chairs and stay low enough that she didn't scrape herself on the table's edge. By the time she slithered back into the open, she could feel her face was red and her hair was a frizzled mess.

Naturally, this was when Madison showed up.

"Looking good, Gabbers!" Madison chirped, a huge smile on her face. "Good news! Everyone's so happy about the cookbook, we're putting you back in the Hooty suit!"

"Wow," Gabby said ruefully, "that *is* good news."

"Isn't it? Now why don't you give me the cookbook so I can lock it up with the rest of the auction items?" Madison's eyes narrowed and though her voice remained peppy, her smile grew cold. "Unless this is all a lie and you don't actually *have* the cookbook to give me."

"Of course she has it," Zee said, stepping between Gabby and Madison, "but she's not going to give it to you *now*. She'll do it at the auction. It's more dramatic that way, in front of your live feed and all. Plus she doesn't trust you to keep it safe."

Madison glared down at Zee, then back at Gabby. "I don't believe you," she said. "I don't think you really have it. But that's okay. If you do, my auction's a success and I win. If you don't, the orchestra hates you more than ever and won't play with you anymore . . . and I win!" She took a deep cleansing breath and pulled herself a little taller. "Thank you, Gabby Duran, for making my day soooo much better."

She turned on her heel and practically floated out of the room.

"You told her I'd give her the book at the auction?" Gabby railed to Zee. "In front of the live feed?"

"I was buying you time!" Zee retorted. "Plus I didn't like the look on her face, all smug and I'm-better-than-Gabby."

Gabby collapsed back into her chair. "I love that you guys stick up for me," she said to Zee and Satchel, "but now I am seriously doomed if I don't get the riddle answer to Trymmy."

"I've got it!" Satchel snapped. "We find a fortune-teller! Then we'll know how this all ends up. If it's bad, we get you on a plane to another country right now."

"This isn't a spy movie," Zee said. "She's not going to another country. Besides, if we had a fortune-teller, the first thing we'd ask is how to give someone 'the future.'"

"A fortune-teller," Gabby mused. "You guys, that's it!"

"It is?" Satchel asked. "'Cause I wasn't actually a hundred percent serious. But if you like the idea . . ."

"I don't like it, I love it!" Gabby smacked her palms on the table and leaned forward, her eyes bright. "I know *exactly* how to give Trymmy the future!"

chapter TWELVE

Gabby had been riding Satchel's delivery bike for the better part of forty-five minutes. He had an after-school-and-weekend job delivering pizzas for his aunt Toni's restaurant and always rode the bike to school so he could start work once classes ended. Even days like today, when H.O.O.T. would keep him from any deliveries until much later, he still preferred the bike to the bus or getting crammed into a car with all his cousins. That's why it was available for Gabby. It was an incredibly cumbersome vehicle, with a brutally heavy metal rack on the back, and Gabby weaved back and forth along the shoulder

of the road, fighting for balance the whole way.

It was the word "fortune-teller" that had done it. Once Gabby heard that, she knew what she needed for Trymmy, and she knew exactly where to get it. Satchel and Zee had offered to accompany her, but the trip there and back on the bike would take the rest of the school day, and she didn't want them to skip classes and risk getting in trouble. It was the same reason Gabby had said no when Zee offered to take them all on the jet-powered surfboard.

Gabby panted heavily and her heart raced, but it was only partially because of the ride. She'd let so many people down lately—Edwina, Trymmy, the orchestra—and now she had a chance to make at least some of it right. She was so desperate to succeed, it left her gasping for air.

Finally, Gabby weaved Satchel's bike into the Square, a shopping area that straddled Brensville and the next town over. It was a great place for hanging out, filled with unique shops and built around a small park, with lots of wide sidewalks. Gabby steered the bike as best she could past coffee shops, yoga studios, and little boutiques, then pulled up to Bottle Rockets, the greatest candy store in the world. Walking in, Gabby faced aisle after aisle of the most unique treats in the universe. Or maybe not in the *whole* universe, but since she was no longer with A.L.I.E.N. Gabby would never really know.

Normally, Gabby would spend hours perusing all the treats. She'd pore over the wall of sodas in bizarre flavors like salty watermelon. She'd stare in awe at the Double Decker bars from England, and the chocobanana, soy sauce, and grilled potato Kit Kats imported from Japan. She'd ponder the merits of an entire aisle of candies made from bacon.

Today, however, she ignored all of that. She wasn't here for candy, she was here for the store's other draw: kitschy toys and memorabilia. These were on round tables scattered between candy stacks. Gabby whizzed past each of them, looking for one specific item amidst the joy buzzers, squeezy stress dolls with bulge-out faces, and Chinese finger traps.

Then she saw it.

A Magic 8 Ball.

She picked it up. The clear fortune-telling window of the ball showed through the square packaging. Gabby looked away and thought hard.

Are you something that represents the future?

She held the package still and waited as an answer floated to the glass surface.

It is decidedly so, it said.

"Yes!" Gabby cried.

She raced to the counter, but when she got there she gasped out loud.

The cashier was a man maybe ten years older than her mom, tall and lean, with a deep tan, crinkles along the sides of his blue eyes, and salt-and-pepper hair. He wore scruffy black jeans and a Bottle Rocket T-shirt. He was good-looking for someone his age, but that wasn't why Gabby gasped. She gasped because she had seen him before. On the playground, dressed in a blazer and watching kids play. On her street, wearing rumpled rags and pushing a shopping cart. In front of a house, pruning bushes.

It was the man she'd dubbed the Silver Fox.

Gabby's brain went a little fuzzy. She hadn't been concerned about the Silver Fox before, but now she was specifically hoping to be around Trymmy. She could *not* have some crazy G.E.T.O.U.T. kook around her when that happened. Gabby had made that mistake once. Never again.

The Silver Fox seemed far more relaxed than Gabby. He smiled. His laugh lines grew deeper.

"Have I seen you before?" he asked.

Gabby didn't like his smile. It looked like the smile of a snake just before it leaped out of its coil and struck. Or like the smile of Madison Murray.

Show no weakness. That, Gabby figured, was the smartest thing to do. If she acted like a totally normal kid who would never even suspect she was being followed, maybe he'd think that's exactly what she was.

"I don't think so," she answered his question. "I'm in a bit of a hurry, though, so if you could just ring me up . . ."

"No problem," he said. As he did, he nodded to a bright yellow piece of paper. Someone from the orchestra had clearly been here with the flyers. "You know anything about this?" he asked. "Brensville Middle School H.O.O.T. Auction?"

Gabby shook her head, staring down at her purchase so she didn't have to look at him as she lied. "Sorry, no. Why?"

The Silver Fox shrugged and handed her a receipt. "You just seem like the right age to know. Word around the store is that the big secret item is a first edition collectible cookbook. Pretty amazing find, right?"

Gabby shrugged. "Not my kind of thing," she said. She stuffed the Magic 8 Ball into her knapsack, ran out the door, hopped clumsily onto Satchel's delivery bike, and pedaled toward school. She looked over her shoulder a few times to see if Silver Fox was following her, but he wasn't. Good.

Between the wobbly bike and her wobbly nerves, Gabby didn't get back until the tail end of eighth period. That meant she missed the bulk of orchestra class time, which everyone was supposed to spend at the gym doing last-minute H.O.O.T. preparations. Gabby got there as fast as she could, and tried to walk in unnoticed. Maybe she could blend in and pretend she'd been there the whole time.

"GABBY!" the whole room chorused.

Gabby waved and returned all their smiles, then sidled next to Satchel.

"They didn't think I was coming, did they?" Gabby asked him under her breath. "They thought I ran off and wouldn't bring the book."

"Every one of them," he agreed under his breath. "They were all cursing your name."

"S'okay," Gabby said with a smile. "I have the future."

"Sweet!" Satchel cried.

"Gabby Duran," Madison called sharply over the on-stage microphone, "I realize time doesn't apply to you, but it's the end of eighth period and we're going to open the doors soon. I suggest you get into your Hooty suit!"

Gabby rolled her eyes. She wanted nothing *less* than to get into the Hooty suit, but it was necessary for her plan to work. Satchel sighed sadly as he handed her the shopping bag containing the giant atrocity, and Gabby lugged it to the girls' locker room. The place smelled about as fresh and clean as the inside of an old sock. The good part about that, Gabby supposed, was that the dank musk inside Hooty's head might feel comparatively refreshing.

Gabby quickly realized she should have brought someone to help her into the costume. She thought the body would slip on like a pair of footy pajamas, but there was so much extra fabric she practically got lost in it. Once she'd

struggled into the limbs and slipped her feet into the uncomfortable plastic flippers, she had to nearly dislocate her arms to fasten the zipper. By the time she put on the head she was already sweaty and exhausted, and she hadn't even started her H.O.O.T. mascot duties.

She peered into a mirror. Hooty's mesh eyeholes gave her a very small field of vision, but her reflection proved what she'd remembered: that there was no way to see it was her inside. If Trymmy *did* show up, he technically wouldn't be seen anywhere near Gabby. That meant A.L.I.E.N. wouldn't know she was breaking their rules, and *that* meant she wouldn't have her memory erased.

Things were coming together. Now she just had to hope that Trymmy actually arrived, that she was able to get him where she needed him to go, and that she'd been correct when she'd figured out the riddle in the first place. Gabby tried to convince herself those were small hurdles to leap.

She strode out into the gym, dangling her knapsack by its straps. Even muffled by the owl head, the roar of the crowd was deafening. Gabby couldn't believe it. In the time she'd been wrestling with her costume, the place had filled. Every chair on the floor was occupied, and plenty of people sat in the bleachers that rose on both sides of the room. Almost everyone held one of the cardboard owl-mask paddles the orchestra had crafted for bidding. Some waved them around, others held them up to their faces, and at any given moment half the audience was hooting.

Gabby smiled inside her giant stuffed head. It was pretty impressive. She hoped things went well.

"Hooty!"

Gabby heard the cry and turned to see her mom, Carmen, and Zee. They sat on the lowest row of bleachers, with Zee and Alice on either side of Carmen. Even though both Alice and Zee were crunched against people on their non-Carmen side, they each sat a good six inches away from Carmen to make sure she had her space. Gabby ran over to them, dragging her knapsack low by her side. It was a dead giveaway to her true identity.

"Gabby, you look so cute!" Alice cried as she fished in her purse. "I need to take your picture."

"Not Gabby," Gabby insisted. "Not here. Just Hooty." She slipped her knapsack to Carmen. "Can you hold this, please?" she asked. "And keep it with you. It's important."

"It's really not," Carmen said. "Not compared to global warming, or unrest in the Middle East, or—"

"It's important to *me*," Gabby clarified. "Please hold on to it." She needed the knapsack to stay safe, since it held the Magic 8 Ball. It also served her to have the bag specifically with Carmen.

Gabby turned her owly face to Zee. "Heard anything?"

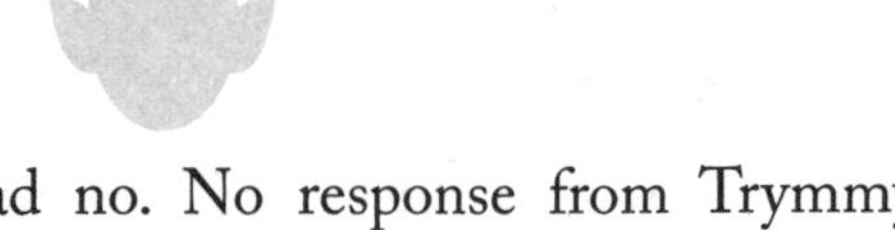

Zee shook her head no. No response from Trymmy. Would he even show?

Just then, Madison's voice rang out through the gym. "Good afternoon, everyone, and welcome to our auction! Can I hear a hoot?"

Madison cupped a hand to her ear, and everyone in the gym (except Carmen) responded with a spirited *"HOOT!"*

"Woo-*hoot*!" Madison cheered in return. She was dressed on theme, in a green dress with leaves of silk for the skirt. A crown of red flowers circled her hair, which hung loose except for one Zee-like braid on either side. She looked like a beautiful woodland fairy, minus the wings, and for a second Gabby wondered where in the world she had changed. She certainly hadn't been with Gabby in the sweaty locker room.

"We'll officially start the auction and live stream in a minute," Madison continued. "We just want to give everyone time to get here and settle in. In the meantime, for your entertainment, I present our mascot, Hooty the H.O.O.T. Owl!

Every eye in the room shifted to Gabby. That's when she realized that in all her frenzy to get ready, she hadn't planned what she'd *do* in the owl suit.

She tried giving her arms a flap.

The room erupted in cheers.

Energized by the crowd's response, she pranced around the room, flapping her wings and leaping as well as she could in the flipper feet. Gabby could hear people roar with laughter, but she *really* knew she was doing a good job when Madison cleared her throat loudly over the microphone.

"Thanks, Hooty! That's all for now. Go sit on your egg."

That got big laughs, too, and Madison kept the crowd's attention by launching into the first item up for bids.

As time passed and Gabby anxiously watched the door for Trymmy, she couldn't help but notice how successfully the auction was going. Bids came in from the crowd in the gym, they came in from online. . . . It seemed like everyone was wrapped up in the energy and wanted a piece of the action. Each item got bids, even the jack-in-the-box, whose pop-up clown didn't have a head. Apparently, an eighth grader named Eric Carlyle thought it would be the perfect instrument for torturing his baby sister.

Still, Gabby understood why Maestro Jenkins had warned Madison against an auction in the first place. Items were selling, but they weren't making a lot of money. Even higher-priced lots like Gabby's night of free babysitting only got two hundred and fifty dollars. Two hundred and fifty dollars was a ridiculously huge amount of money for a night of sitting, but the orchestra needed ten thousand dollars to

make it to MusicFest, and the tote board with their running total was nowhere near that number.

Gabby was about to stroll her owly self outside to see if Trymmy was anywhere near the building, when something so terrible caught her eye that if she could have laid an egg, she would have.

Someone new was sitting next to her mother.

Someone Gabby recognized. A very charming-looking middle-aged man with a tan, laugh lines, and salt-and-pepper hair. He wore broken-in jeans and a blue T-shirt that brought out his startlingly blue eyes.

It was the Silver Fox. With a wide smile, he leaned close to Alice Duran and whispered something in her ear. She threw back her head and laughed, then looked around conspiratorially before whispering something back to him that he clearly found terribly amusing.

Holy fricassoli.

Were her mom and the Silver Fox *flirting*???

For a second Gabby stopped breathing. This was a bad choice not only for the obvious reason, but because when she started up again she had to take a very deep breath of noxious owl-head must.

A G.E.T. O.U.T. agent flirting with her mom? Using her mom to get to her? Gabby didn't care who she did or didn't

work for anymore, this was unacceptable. She marched as stridently as her flipper-feet would let her and loomed over the Silver Fox, hands on her hips.

"What do you think you're doing?" she snapped.

If the Silver Fox was surprised to find a giant owl yelling at him, he didn't show it.

"Hooty!" Alice cried happily. "I was hoping you'd get a chance to come over. This is Arlington. Arlington, this is Hooty the H.O.O.T. Owl." She dropped her voice to a stage whisper. "Actually it's my other daughter, Gabby." She put her fingers to her lips, warning him to keep silent about it.

He nodded solemnly and his voice was soft. "Gabby Duran . . . I think I've read something about you."

"In the local papers, I'm sure," Alice said. "Gabby had a big solo last week in the orchestra's fall concert."

"That must be it," the Silver Fox said, though Gabby was sure he'd actually read about her on the G.E.T.O.U.T. secured Web site. She glared daggers at him, then realized all he was seeing was the cross-eyed demented smile of Hooty the H.O.O.T. Owl.

"It's so funny Arlington sat here," Alice said. "He used to write for *Fabulous Foods* magazine. I've read his articles! Isn't it amazing that of all the places in the gym he happened to sit down next to me?"

"Amazing," Carmen deadpanned.

Gabby's thought exactly. She had to get this man away from her mom, but how?

"Hooty!" cried Madison from the podium. "Have we lost our mascot?"

The last thing Gabby felt like doing was a Hooty bit right now, but then she got an idea. She grabbed the microphone from Lilah Hartmann, who was taking bids at one of the computers, and called, "I'm right here, Madison, and this time I'm doing a great big Hooty the H.O.O.T. Owl Dance with a lucky member of our audience! Hit it!"

"What?!" Madison spluttered. "Hooty, you're not supposed to speak! And we don't have dance music for—"

But Zee had Gabby's back. She had already hopped up, pulled out her phone, and plugged it into the amp system. Hip-hop music blared, and Gabby started a ridiculous dance, flapping her wings and waggling her tail feathers. The crowd loved it and clapped along. Gabby then pointed a wing at Silver Fox. He shook his head as if embarrassed, but Gabby danced his way, pulled him up by the hand, and spun him onto the floor, *far* away from Alice. He danced gamely along with Hooty, then Gabby pulled in another volunteer: Alana Mulloney, a waitress at Toni's. Alana's ex-husband had just remarried, and she'd been telling everyone in the restaurant that it was her turn to find someone. Gabby knew she would go nuts for a handsome guy like the Silver Fox.

Sure enough, Alana threw one arm around Silver Fox's waist, took his hand, and led him across the floor in a wild tango he could only try to follow. Gabby waved her wings in the air to get the crowd cheering. They roared.

"That's enough of that!" Madison cried. "Don't want to keep our online viewers waiting too long between bids. Next up is a three-pack of personalized sessions with nutritionist Sheila Cormsby, redeemable in person or online. Do I hear one hundred and fifty dollars?"

Gabby flapped her way to Zee and told her to cut the music, then said, "You have to keep that guy busy. He's G.E.T.O.U.T. I don't want him near my mom, and if Trymmy and his parents come, I need him far away from them."

"On it," Zee said. "I know exactly what to do, just need a little time."

"No problem," Gabby said. "I'll get Satch."

She raced up the bleachers to Satchel, who was back on his original duty.

"Recycling collection!" he called down rows. "If you've got recycling, I'm collecting it!"

Several cans and bottles flew toward him. Satchel ducked and lunged acrobatically to catch them in his large blue bin.

"I need your help," Gabby told him. "See that guy?" She pointed out Silver Fox, who had already settled back into his

seat next to Alice. "I need you to keep him far away from my mom. Can you help me?"

Satchel considered. "Can I tell him I'm with the CDC and we need to quarantine him because we believe he's been exposed to a rare and deadly contagious virus?"

"You can," Gabby said, "but he might not believe you. Maybe something a little more school-centric."

"Got it," Satchel said. He put down his bin, straightened his shirt, and raced excitedly across the gym. "Congratulations!" Satchel cried, pumping the Silver Fox's hand up and down. "You're in seat number four hundred and twenty-eight A! That means you win a special behind-the-scenes tour of the Brensville Middle School gymnasium!"

"No, thank you," Silver Fox demurred. "I'd rather not. I was just up, and—"

"Oh, go on," Alice said, laughing. "It's all part of the fun."

Gabby smiled inside her suit, watching Silver Fox's discomfort. If he wanted to keep up his charade of being an innocent, charming guy, he had no choice but to obey. Gabby relished the way Silver Fox's back hunched in defeat as Satchel led him up the bleachers, prattling brilliantly about nothing.

"So if you count the steps to the top of the bleachers, you'll see they're actually representative of the number of athletes Brensville Middle School has sent to the Olympics over the years. An interesting choice, since if we send any more, we'll have to add more stairs and possibly raise the ceiling. . . ."

Satchel's tour took care of the Silver Fox for quite a while. By the time the so-called Arlington collapsed back in his seat next to Alice, Zee was ready. She had run out of the gym after speaking with Gabby, only to return to her seat next to Carmen, this time carrying her camouflage duffel bag. When no one was looking, Zee took out a small cylindrical robot that moved on tanklike wheeled tracks. Once Zee placed it on the floor, the robot zipped past Carmen, past Alice, and came to a stop under Arlington's chair. Then it reached up one wiry arm and used its gripper fingers to unclasp the Silver Fox's watch. The robot carefully eased the watch off Arlington's wrist, then zoomed at top speed down the floor.

"Wilbur!" Zee shouted loud enough for Arlington to hear. She leaned over Alice and Carmen to tell the Silver Fox, "I'm so sorry. I was testing Wilbur's stealth grip, and I think he took your watch!"

"Who?" Arlington said. "My what?"

"Your *robot* Wilbur?" Alice asked.

Zee nodded. "I'm really sorry."

By then Arlington had looked at his wrist and felt it, as if the watch might be there and he just didn't see it. "I don't . . . Where did it . . ."

"Over there!" Zee cried, pointing to Wilbur scooting unnoticed under legs and chairs as it zoomed at top speed toward the far end of the gym. Arlington leaped up to give chase, and Zee grinned with satisfaction as he scrambled hopelessly after the speedy robot. Gabby noticed Zee fidgeting with her hands and wondered if Wilbur's remote controls were tucked away in one of her palms.

While Satchel and Zee handled the Silver Fox, Gabby kept busy. She did her Hooty routine whenever Madison asked, but mostly she watched for Trymmy.

There was no sign of him.

Gabby stayed hopeful, but that got harder the more time passed.

All too soon, the list of items up for bids dwindled down to just a few. The auction was hurtling to a close, and Gabby had to face the facts.

Trymmy wasn't coming.

Gabby had failed.

The minute she realized it, all the energy drained out of her. She didn't want to be a happily dancing owl anymore, she just wanted to be alone. She slunk to a far wall near the gymnasium door and slid down it.

All her life, Gabby had cared the most about just a few things: her friends, her family, babysitting, and her music. She put tons of energy into all those things, and they all

thrived. She had a great relationship with her mom and Carmen, she and Zee and Satchel were inseparable, she was a terrific babysitter, and she played French horn like no one she had ever met.

Working for A.L.I.E.N. was the first new thing Gabby had cared about in forever. She'd cared about it deeply. She'd only gotten to sit for three alien kids, but each one of them was incredibly special, and they'd trusted her to keep this huge secret that meant everything to their very existence. She'd wanted so badly to be worthy of that trust, and she'd worked really hard to do a great job, but for the first time ever, that wasn't enough. She'd failed. She'd lost the position she loved. Now all she wanted more than anything was to make one little boy's life better—and she knew exactly how to do it!—but she wouldn't get the chance.

She was about to take off her head, slip out the door, and go home, when she heard a voice next to her.

"Why are you hiding back here? Don't you *give a hoot* about the auction?"

Gabby wheeled her stuffed head around.

It was Trymmy. His mouth was curled in a sidelong smile, pleased at his joke. Allynces and Feltrymm stood just behind him. They looked around at the decorations distastefully.

Gabby couldn't believe it. She inwardly thanked herself

for not pulling off the Hooty head. Allynces and Feltrymm never would have let her get away with what she was about to do if she weren't a giant, friendly-looking owl. She grabbed Trymmy's hand with her wing and pulled him down the line of bleachers. He resisted at first.

"Hey! What are you doing? Let go of me."

"It's me," she said through the mouth hole. "Gabby."

"Gabby?"

"Shhh."

She noticed that neither Silver Fox nor Zee was anywhere to be seen, which was good. Zee must still have him on a wild-goose chase to find his watch. Gabby pulled Trymmy all the way to her knapsack, which sat in front of Carmen. Adrenaline and clumsy wings made it almost impossible for her to pry open the zipper, but she finally managed. With a breathless flourish, she pulled out her recent purchase and held it out to Trymmy.

"A Magic 8 Ball," he said. "Cool."

"It's not just 'cool,' it's the answer to your riddle: 'the future'!"

"But 'the future' isn't the answer," Trymmy said.

"Sure it is!" Gabby insisted. "'I never was, am always to be'—the future. 'No one ever saw me, nor ever will see'—the future. 'I can't be bought, I can't be sold'—the future."

"You can sell futures in the stock market," Carmen said. Gabby hadn't realized her sister had been paying attention.

"You can?" Gabby asked.

"You can," Trymmy said.

"And is that the whole riddle?" Carmen asked.

"No," Trymmy replied. "It ends, 'The young have more of me than the old. And yet I am the hope of all, who live and breathe on your terrestrial ball.'"

Carmen shrugged. "The answer's 'tomorrow.'"

Trymmy smiled. "Yeah. It is." He extended a formal hand toward Carmen. "I'm Trymmy."

Carmen didn't take it. "Carmen. Got any more riddles?"

"You have no idea."

"I have *some* idea. There's a limited permutation of words in the English language."

"What if I speak another language?" Trymmy asked.

Carmen thought a minute. "I'd need more data." She gestured to the spot next to her that Zee had vacated. "You can sit if you want. Just not too close."

On Carmen's other side, Alice had been watching this curiously, and now she clapped a hand over her mouth to stop from gasping out loud. Gabby understood why. Carmen didn't invite *anyone* to sit down and talk to her. Social overtures weren't generally her thing.

Allynces and Feltrymm had been running after Trymmy.

They caught up now, just as Trymmy took a seat next to, but several inches away from, Carmen.

"You can't run off like that, Trymmy!" Allynces snapped, but she didn't get anything else out before Alice jumped up to effusively introduce herself.

"Are you Trymmy's parents?" she asked. "I'm Alice Duran. It is *wonderful* to meet you."

Gabby had been so entranced by Trymmy and Carmen hitting it off that she hadn't seen this coming. Fire smoldered in Allynces's eyes as she turned from Alice to Gabby. "Alice . . . *Duran*?" she asked.

"Yes," Alice said, not realizing the sudden temperature drop in the room. "That's my daughter Carmen, and *this*"—she gestured to the owl suit—"is my other daughter, Gabby."

Both Feltrymm and Allynces were fuming now. With her identity blown, and the Silver Fox nowhere in sight, Gabby went ahead and pulled off the owl head. It was a massive relief to gasp fresh air, even though she was sure her face was bright red, her hair was everywhere, and her head smelled like the inside of a sweat sock.

"I can explain," she said.

"GABBY DURAN!" Madison squealed from the podium. "I'm so glad you revealed yourself, because we're down to one last item. Please bring us what we've all been waiting for . . . the cookbook!"

"Right, the cookbook!" Gabby called out. Then she turned to Trymmy. "Carmen answered the riddle. You can give me the cookbook now, right?"

"*Carmen* answered the riddle," Trymmy said. "You didn't. The book stays with me. Those are the rules."

"You have to play by the rules, Gabby," Carmen agreed.

Allynces leaned down and took Trymmy's arm. "Trymmy, let's go. We're leaving."

"So soon?" Alice asked.

"Yes," she insisted, then turned to Gabby. "And *you* will be facing the stiffest punishment from our mutual acquaintances, I assure you."

"GABBY!" Madison cried.

Gabby heard the voice, but through a fog.

So that was it. On top of everything else, Gabby was going to lose her memories. She wouldn't remember Wutt, or Philip, or Trymmy.

If A.L.I.E.N. was at all merciful, she wouldn't remember Madison, either.

"GABBY DURAN, YOU LISTEN TO ME RIGHT NOW!" Madison wailed through the microphone, making it screech with feedback.

"I don't have the cookbook, okay?" Gabby shouted loud enough for her to hear. "I don't have it!"

A murmur of disbelief spread through the gym.

"Really, Gabby?" Madison boomed from the stage. "We still need two thousand dollars, which the cookbook could easily get. Are you telling me you're going to fail the orchestra so we can't go to MusicFest?"

"Yes, that's exactly what I'm telling you," she replied. "Auction's over."

Somewhere, dimly, Gabby understood that people were shouting things to and about her, and the crowd was breaking up and getting ready to go. Gabby didn't care about any of it. Only one thing was on her mind. She wanted to come through for Trymmy, even if she was doomed to forget every moment of what she'd done.

Using both owl wings, she pulled Allynces by the arm.

"Get off me!" Allynces cried, batting at Gabby's wings, but Gabby held on so she could say her piece.

"Mrs. Vyllsk . . . Mrs. Villis . . ." Gabby gave up trying to remember her last name and just called her by her first. "Allynces," she began again, keeping her voice low so Trymmy wouldn't hear and be embarrassed, "I know what's going to happen to me, and honestly, I'm fine with it. I deserve it. I messed up, and probably you're all safer if I don't remember anything about any of you. But please. Don't take Trymmy away just yet. Did you know he spent all his free time at Lion's Gate Academy hiding in the Lost and Found?"

"I'm aware," she said coldly. "Humans aren't kind to those who look different."

"*Some* humans aren't kind. But maybe Trymmy only had no friends because he never found the right people. Just look. *Please.*"

She pointed toward Carmen and Trymmy, who were speaking in machine-gun blasts back and forth as if there were no one else in the gym. Neither Alice nor Feltrymm could take their eyes off them.

Allynces was looking now, too. Slowly, she moved closer and Gabby followed.

"You shouldn't like riddles so much," Carmen said. "They're easy. Puzzles are hard."

"*Riddles* are hard," Trymmy said. "They take razor-sharp mental acuity."

Carmen shrugged. "They take logic. What's bought by the yard and worn by the foot?"

"A carpet," Trymmy answered. "The man who invented it doesn't want it. The man who bought it doesn't need it. The man who needs it doesn't know it. What is it?"

"A coffin," Carmen said. "A thing there is whose voice is one; whose feet are four and two and three. So mutable a thing is none that moves in earth or sky or sea. When on most feet this thing doth go, its strength is weakest and its pace most slow. What is it?"

"It's a . . ."

Gabby, Alice, Allynces, and Feltrymm had been watching the volley like a tennis match, and they all held their breath as something flickered in Trymmy's eyes. He pulled himself a little taller and arched his unibrow knowingly.

"It's a . . ."

The knowing look faded. He tipped a mole into his mouth and sucked on it as he contemplated. Then he grinned.

"I don't know," he said.

"You don't?" Gabby asked.

"Nope." He turned to Carmen. "What is it?"

"A person," Carmen said. "One voice, but the feet change. Four feet as a crawling baby, two feet when he can walk, three when he's old and needs a cane. The more feet, the slower and weaker he is. Even an old man with a cane can get around faster and lift more than a crawling baby."

Trymmy's grin spread even wider. "Yeah, that's true, but I didn't get it. You stumped me. Hey, want to play Secret Mega Orbs?" He pulled two marbles out of his pocket, then looked at Gabby. "Can I grab more orbs?"

Gabby nodded, and Trymmy dug into her knapsack to pull out the sack of marbles.

Trymmy's mother turned to Alice. "I'm afraid I didn't introduce myself. Allynces Vyllskryn. This is my husband Feltrymm. And our son, Trymmy."

Alice, Allynces, and Feltrymm kept talking, but Gabby didn't hear it because she was distracted by a scream in her ear.

"What is wrong with you, Gabby Duran?!" Madison wailed. Gabby saw she now looked less like a woodland fairy and more like a volcano about to erupt.

"Madison, I'm sorry about the book."

"The one that's sitting at your feet?!" Madison shrieked.

Gabby looked down. Sure enough, a thick greenish-colored tattered volume of *Joy of Cooking* sat on the floor in front of her.

Of course! Carmen had stumped Trymmy with a riddle! Everything he'd ever stolen would be returned to its rightful owners! Gabby's heart leaped as she scooped the book into her hands and presented it to Madison.

"Yes, this one!" she cried. "I have it right here! Let's auction it off and get to MusicFest!"

"Are you insane?!" Madison wailed. "Look around you! Everyone left! You said it was over! The online people logged off! It's *done*!"

Gabby looked around. Madison was right. The gym that had been teeming with people a few minutes ago was now practically empty. No one manned the dark computer tables. No one sat in the chairs on the floor. A small group of Madison's friends huddled by the stage, and only a few stray knots of students and parents dotted the gym floor and bleachers.

"Great work, Gabby," she sniped. "Thanks to you, we missed MusicFest by two thousand dollars. Good luck having anything to do with anyone in orchestra after this."

"Two thousand dollars, you say?" Feltrymm piped up.

Gabby hadn't even realized that he, Allynces, and Alice had stopped talking, but all three of them were now focused on Gabby and Madison. Madison had clearly also not known she was under parental scrutiny. She straightened out her green dress, stood a little taller, and tried to put on a good face for her audience.

"Yes, that's exactly what I'm saying. And it's all Gabby's fault."

"We bid five thousand for the cookbook," Allynces said.

Madison looked like she'd been whomped in the face with the world's largest pillow. "*Five* thousand dollars?"

"Yes," Feltrymm agreed. "That should cover everything with a little extra padding."

Allynces dug into her purse. "To whom should I make out the check?"

"The Help Our Orchestra Travel Fund," Madison said in a daze. When Allynces handed her the check she added, "Thank you. Thank you very much."

Then Madison wheeled away from the group and held the check in the air. "I did it!" she screamed. "I got the money! We're going to MusicFest!"

The small knot of Madison's besties turned and squealed. They raced toward Madison, who met them at the center of the room. "We have to get Maestro and tell him—*I* saved our trip!"

Together, the girls ran out of the gym.

"I don't understand at all," Alice said, her brows knitted. "Gabby, you told me you lost the book."

Thankfully, Gabby didn't have to answer. The sound of pounding feet took her attention, and she wheeled around to see a red-faced and breathless Satchel and Zee burst in across the gym. She excused herself and raced over to them.

"Wilbur was running low on power, so we had to stop Silver Fox another way," Zee said in a fast, panting whisper.

"She had the robot lead him to the laundry room and we locked him in," Satchel added.

"But he's out now and he's coming this way!" Zee finished.

That's when Gabby heard more stomping feet. The Silver Fox had emerged from the bowels of the gymnasium and was storming, head down, toward Allynces, Feltrymm, and Trymmy.

No. Gabby would *not* let this G.E.T.O.U.T. agent anywhere near the Trolls. She waddled across the floor as fast as her flippered feet would let her. The Silver Fox noticed her when she was still several feet away. "Oh," he said with a friendly smile. "Hello."

Instead of responding, Gabby threw herself onto her stomach, for the first time grateful that Madison had made her wear a giant carpet. The owl suit skated across the shiny, slick gymnasium floor, and Gabby covered her face with her wings as her body barreled into the Silver Fox's legs and knocked him to the ground. He sprawled forward. When he rolled onto his back to get his bearings, Gabby was right there, leaning over him to stare down into his face.

"There's no way I'm letting you use my mom to get to me," she said menacingly, "and if you think I don't know who you are, you're crazy."

"Who am I?" he asked frantically.

"G.E.T.O.U.T." Gabby hissed.

"I would love to, but you're on top of me!"

"What is going on?" Alice cried, walking their way. "Gabby, are you okay? Arlington?"

She held out her hand to the Silver Fox and helped him up while Gabby rose to her owl-feet. "You can't trust this man, Mom. He said he writes for a magazine? I saw him selling candy at Bottle Rockets."

Arlington's face brightened as he smiled and nodded. "Yes! You're the girl who came in to buy the Magic 8 Ball. I didn't recognize you with the owl head on. And I said I *did* write for a magazine. Now I'm working on a novel. I'm afraid I have a quirky habit of living like my characters to get inside

their heads. I've worked at the candy store, as a gardener, in a law office . . . I even spent a day as a homeless man just to make sure the details I wrote were real."

"That's remarkable," Alice said.

Her eyes shone with admiration, and Arlington looked down at her with equal fondness.

Gabby's stomach rolled over. Was her mom seriously falling for this guy's story? Not that it was an unreasonable story. It kind of made sense. And Gabby certainly didn't have *proof* that Arlington was with G.E.T.O.U.T. It wasn't like he was chasing down the Trolls, who were only sitting half a gym away.

Still, for whatever reason, Gabby felt queasy watching the two of them. That she knew.

"Gabs?" Zee said softly. "You okay? You look a little pale."

Gabby realized Zee and Satchel were both looking at her worriedly. She smiled. "Yeah. I just need a second. I'll be right back."

She flippered her way to the girls' locker room and headed for the stalls. She didn't think she'd actually throw up, but better safe than sorry. She pulled open a stall door, then backed away screaming.

"Hello, Gabby," Edwina said.

The woman was standing stock-still, right there in front of the toilet. As always, she was dressed all in black and wore

an expression of pure business. As if lurking in a bathroom stall was a perfectly normal part of her day.

Gabby took a deep breath. Now that the shock had worn off, she knew exactly why Edwina was here, and she supposed she was ready. She stood taller and tried to look dignified in her owl body.

"Just promise me it won't hurt," she said.

"What exactly do you not wish to hurt?" Edwina asked.

"Aren't you going to erase my memory?"

"That was meant to be my assignment, yes," Edwina said. "We've of course been keeping an eye on you and knew you were going to defy direct orders. But then things changed."

"They did?"

"Indeed. My superiors received a very forceful text message from Allynces. She not only insisted that you remain affiliated with A.L.I.E.N., but she has already booked your services for the next three Wednesdays after school."

"Booked me to babysit?" Gabby asked. "But doesn't that mean . . . ?"

A hint of a smile played on Edwina's lips. "The Unsittables program is officially back in business."

"It is?" Gabby was elated, but also confused. "And I'm still in it? Even after I went against your orders, and led G.E.T.O.U.T. to Trymmy, and—"

"You made mistakes," Edwina said, "but you also acted out of great love and respect for another being, even though it meant putting the memories you value at risk. Nothing speaks more to the mission of A.L.I.E.N."

Edwina leaned down a bit to look Gabby in the eye, and Gabby was surprised to see Edwina's own eyes were a little misty. "Allow me to add that I am very proud of you, Gabby, and it is a personal honor to reinstate you as Associate 4118-25125A. Well done."

Gabby flushed with pride. "Thank you."

"By bringing Trymmy to your sister, you also did quite a service to humanity. You'll recall Trymmy's collection encompassed items from his grandfather's thieveries as well as his own. Thanks to Carmen's riddle, they're now all back with their rightful owners. At this very moment, for example, researchers are going quite apoplectic over the sudden discovery of Amelia Earhart's lost plane." Edwina clip-clopped toward a back door that Gabby was quite sure hadn't existed the last time she was in the room.

"There's also an item that you, in particular, might find interesting," Edwina added. "I suggest you check your pockets."

With that, she pushed open the door and left.

Gabby tried to obey, but she couldn't reach her pockets through the owl costume. With her hands still covered by a layer of wing, she fought to unzip the back, then let the

costume slip down to the floor. As she stepped out of the flippers, she reached inside the pockets of her jeans.

Her right hand touched something hard and flat.

She pulled it out. It was a silver rectangle with rounded corners, attached to a chain of beaded metal. A second rounded rectangle dangled from the other end of the chain.

Dog tags. Military dog tags. Gabby held them up to look more closely, and the name on them stopped her heart.

Steven Duran.

Gabby's father. He'd gone missing in action when Carmen was a baby. His body was never found.

How had Trymmy's grandfather ended up with his dog tags?

"Edwina! Edwina!" Gabby raced out the door after her. The outdoor chill blasted Gabby's face, but she didn't even notice. She ran over the grass and into the street, calling Edwina's name and looking for the limo, but it wasn't there.

Edwina was gone.

Now Gabby felt the cold. She tried to go back the way she came, but the door was once again gone. Instead she circled around and walked through the gym's main entrance. She could see everyone from here. Carmen and Trymmy hadn't moved; they were still playing with the marbles. Allynces, Feltrymm, Alice, and Arlington had pulled out a circle of folding chairs and now chatted like old friends.

Zee had powered Wilbur back up, and she and Satchel were maneuvering the robot through an obstacle course of woodland decorations.

Gabby had a million questions. About her dad and Trymmy's grandfather, about Arlington, about what came next for her and A.L.I.E.N. Yet as she looked at the group in the gym, she knew she'd have time for all that later. When Edwina came for her again, Gabby would be ready. In the meantime . . .

Gabby looked at her father's name on the dog tags. Smiling, she hugged her hand around them, slipped them into her pocket, and walked out to join the group. She was thrilled she wouldn't lose her old memories, but she was more excited than ever to make some new ones.

Acknowledgments

We are extraterrestrially excited to continue Gabby's adventures, but no secret dossier happens without the help of enough people to fill the files of A.L.I.E.N. itself. First and foremost, we owe an enormous THANK-YOU to everyone at Hyperion. We are completely humbled by your dedication to Gabby Duran, and all that you've done and continue to do to get her stories out to the world. We are truly eternally grateful.

More specifically, we want to heap a galactic-sized shower of appreciation onto Kieran Viola! Kieran is the most amazing cheerleader, supporter, champion, and friend to us; plus she's also a staggeringly brilliant editor. She has an eagle eye for story and character, no doubt because she's an author in her own right, and you should all check out her books, which she writes as Kieran Scott and Kate Brian. That's right, she has aliases—of course she's the perfect editor for us.

Huge thanks also to Emily Meehan. Emily, you're the reason we're at Hyperion, and we're so thankful you fell in love with Gabby and believed in her right away.

Julie Moody, thank you for your editorial eye; and thank you, Marci Senders and Sarah Not, for your incredible cover ideas and artwork. To our copy editor Jody Corbett, thanks for saving us from all the mistakes we make that we're too close to see. Jamie Baker, we can't ever rave enough about your publicity genius. The swag you made for book one has us doing giddy dances to this day. We loved meeting you in person at the L.A. kickoff, and can't wait to see you again!

Elke Villa, Holly Nagel, and Molly Kong, thank you for your boundless enthusiasm and passion for Gabby. With the three of you in her corner, she can't help but succeed!

Jane Startz, without you there would be no Gabby, and—even more tragically—the two of us never would have met. Thanks for bringing us together and for all your constant hard work and support. Thanks also to Kane Lee and Jake Holm for all your help along the way.

Annette Van Duren and Matthew Saver, agent and lawyer extraordinaire, thank you for working tirelessly on our behalf. We can never thank you enough.

Finally—and this one's really cool—thanks to everyone at Disney Channel for OPTIONING GABBY FOR TELEVISION!!!!! It's still early, so we can't say much about what the Gabby show will be, but it's in Team Mouse's capable hands, and we can't wait to see what they come up with!!!!

Now the personal stuff. It's not a book until Elise thanks her husband, Randy; daughter, Maddie; and dog, Jack-Jack, for their constant support, love, and treat mongering. Thanks also to all her friends and family, and a special shout-out to early readers Rahm Jethani, Grant Yabuki, and Everett Nellis; to Mrs. Finklestein's 2015–2016 third grade class at Carpenter Community Charter for totally adopting book one; and to the kids at CHIME Charter and their wonderful librarian, Heidi Mark, for their excitement about Gabby and her adventures.

Daryle would like to profusely thank Liz Lehmans, Jeannie Hayden, Suzanne Downs, Karen Miller, Wes Hurley, and Bob and Nancy Young for all of their support and encouragement, and Jack Brummet and Keelin Curran for their help in making the Gabby project happen. She'd also like to thank Dan Elenbaas for the opportunity to create Gabby in the first place, and Farai Chideya for putting Gabby in Jane Startz's able hands. To Cynthia True, Erik Wiese, and Marya Sea Kaminski, thanks for always helping with the tough decisions and giving your advice so generously.

But the biggest thank-you of all goes to YOU—every single person who picks up a Gabby Duran book and dives in. We've been lucky enough to meet a bunch of you, and nothing makes us happier. Thanks for joining us on another Gabby adventure; keep reaching out and saying hi, because we love to hear from you, and we hope you'll join us soon for yet another secret dossier about the adventures of Gabby Duran!

Much love always,
Elise and Daryle